The Fata
Morgana Books

The Fata Morgana Books

Jonathan Littell
Translated by Charlotte Mandell

Two Lines Press

Études copyright © 2007, *Récit sur rien* copyright © 2009,
En pièces copyright © 2010, and *Une vieille histoire* copyright © 2012,
all by Jonathan Littell
Translation © 2013 by Charlotte Mandell

Published by Two Lines Press
582 Market Street, Suite 700, San Francisco, CA 94104
www.twolinespress.com

ISBN 978-1-931883-34-4

Library of Congress Control Number: 2013936923

Design by Ragina Johnson
Cover design by Gabriele Wilson
Cover Photo by Matt Henry/Gallery Stock
French Voices Logo designed by Serge Bloch

Printed in the United States of America

This work, published as part of a program providing publication assistance, received
financial support from the French Ministry of Foreign Affairs, the Cultural
Services of the French Embassy in the United States, and FACE (French American
Cultural Exchange). This project is also supported in part by an award from the
National Endowment for the Arts.

ART WORKS.
arts.gov

Contents

Etudes

A Summer Sunday

Down below rise the two towers. They are outlined against a grey sky, mournful from suppressed light. Some trees partly obscure the second one, the one burnt from bottom to top. They stand silent as sentinels, indifferent to everything happening at their feet. The wind rustles the leaves in the trees. Trails of clouds flow lazily across the sky. It's a summer Sunday. After a while, the sun reaches the balcony and warms face and legs. Then for a few hours you take refuge in the dark, cool interior of the apartment.

Opposite, to the left, slanting up the hill, lie the little white patches of the gravestones, a streak scattered between the houses. Above the cemetery stands a handsome dwelling, a large nineteenth century house with imposing wings and columns flanking the main door. Perhaps it was the access to the cemetery. It's difficult to know, as no one can go up there. At night, near that house, there is a light like a fiery gap in the darkness. Again, no one knows who put it there. There are people who must know, but I don't know those people.

Once, I visited a house not too far from that cemetery. It was also on a Sunday, around midday. B. had brought me there, to deliver a package to the residents. We had lingered on the terrace for half an hour, drinking beer with the father, while the daughter cut roses in the garden for B. We were sitting back a little, because the edge of the terrace was exposed. The town stretched out under our feet, with the two towers facing us for once, beneath a blue summer sky veering to white. A few shells were falling somewhere near the General's Residence. We were, the father told me, a mere hundred and fifty meters from the cemetery; I found this information astonishing. Yesterday, he continued, a woman had been killed just below his house, by a shell. The day before had in fact been a very bad day, many people had been killed. But that Sunday I didn't yet know how bad the previous day had been. It was such a beautiful weekend. On Saturday, I was having lunch in a café when the General's Residence had been attacked a first time. A piece of shrapnel had bounced in front of my table, with a little clink, and I had run over to pick it up; I came back into the café laughing, tossing the still burning shard from hand to hand, like a roast potato fresh from the oven. Later on, toward the end of the afternoon, I went to some friends' house for cocktails. We were drinking in the garden when rockets came screaming overhead. Several of my friends dove for cover and huddled in a ball at the foot of the rosebushes. It was very funny and we had laughed a lot. The next morning another shell exploded in the garden next door, some fifty meters away from where we had been drinking.

That Sunday, then, after the beer near the cemetery, I accompanied B. to meet our friend A. and we went out to lunch at a beautiful, somewhat isolated restaurant with a terrace only half enclosed, which allowed one to stay out in the open air without breaking police regulations too much. We had eaten slowly, all afternoon, lamb chops with an onion salad, and drank a bottle of red wine. Afterwards, B. and I shared a cigar, too dry but a great pleasure nonetheless. Then we had bought some cakes and gone over for drinks on my balcony, opposite the cemetery with the two towers at our feet. It wasn't till the next day, reading the papers, that we realized just how bad the weekend had been. But the summer had been like that for six weeks already, and it seemed likely it would continue.

The city had been completely closed since the end of May. In fact there was one road to leave and enter, but it was dangerous. This locked-up feeling made some people nervous, but I enjoyed it. I loved the idea of being stuck here all summer, with the heat and the light, being hunted all over the city by the shrill whistle of the mortar shells and the obscene noise of their detonations. It made me enormously fragile and nailed me to that other thing I shouldn't talk about.

That other thing, it's impossible for me to talk about it but it's also impossible for me not to talk about it. It ravaged my heart and ate away at my nights: in the morning, when I woke up, it filled my body and twisted it with happiness. Then I would get up, get dressed, go to my office and get on with my work with a fevered attention that would set it aside for a while. But sometimes the shelling was too heavy, impossible to work, and then between the fear and this thing a vast laziness would overwhelm me, making any effort useless. All that remained then was the balcony, the

5

sun, books, alcohol and the little cigars I went to so much trouble to get, and sometimes also the telephone, for hours on end, a detestable, false solution, but which in the absence of her face and her body fed my anguish and sense of futility. There, I'm talking about it, when I shouldn't. I should talk about something else. Describe things, as in the beginning of this story, describe the pale little cigar I'm smoking right now, the burnished pewter lighter set in front of me, slightly scratched by some coins I had in my pocket, the sky veering to grey. The windows in my office, in order to protect us from possible glass shards, are covered with translucent, self-adhesive plastic sheets; through these sheets, made blotchy by bubbles of air, everything is blurred. It's unfortunate, but on the other hand there is nothing to see opposite my office, just another grey building, dirty, with very few windows intact, and shrapnel streaks across its façade. Ah, the sun has come back, graciously shedding light on that awful façade. There's no denying it, the sun is full of kindness for the poor things of this world.

Earlier in the same notebook in which I'm writing this, I wrote a few weeks ago one or two sentences about the sunlight on B.'s neck. That was also, what a coincidence, on a Sunday (but it's not entirely a coincidence, since I work to justify my presence here, and only the Sundays are left free for such stories). It was one of the most frighteningly painful moments I've known these past few years. What prevented me from kissing her, at that moment? My entire body and all my thought, so weak, were straining toward one thing only: to lay my lips on that neck, dazzling with light and whiteness. What horror. I didn't move, I remained leaning on the rail, then we left. I could blame my natural timidity, but something tells me that would be wrong, a pathetic way out. I think it was more a matter of fear, which isn't the same thing. Beneath that alarming light, so close to her skin, I crumbled, crucified by desire and fear, and I didn't even call out *Eli, Eli,* we chatted, then we left, I picked her a flower, yet another one for the grave of my desire, and I escorted her home.

Really, I shouldn't be talking about these things. The summer goes on, it's far from over. One shouldn't talk about it until afterward, long afterward. The best thing would be never to talk about it, to croak in silence and let all that disappear at the same time, all that tearing apart and that light that in the end you will see life was made of, if you don't see it already, and if it can ever be said of a life that it was made, but if you can't manage to be silent, at least let it come later, and let it be properly digested before you regurgitate it. The summer isn't even over, the sirens have just started wailing, you should learn to grow yourself a skin before you play at scraping it with razors of such poor quality. So much impatience fills me with despair.

– SUMMER 1995

The Wait

So I went back to Paris and waited. It wasn't that I enjoyed waiting, far from it. But there were certain constraints. Normally, I would have left again right away, or after a few days. I'd been offered a post in another country, a harsh and cold country, and that hadn't displeased me, I had readily accepted. But there was a problem with the paperwork, and it wasn't settled yet. My employers already had a man in the capital of that country and it was up to him to solve the problem; I didn't know what he was up to. I telephoned him often, him or his assistant, and there was always an excuse, usually vague, often contradictory; as for the paperwork, nothing. This didn't bother him, he let things follow their course. As for me, I was quietly going crazy.

It had been over a month now that I had been waiting. A month, what is that? Nothing, in some cases; the crossing of an icy marshland, in others. Had they said to me right off the bat, Look, you have to wait a month, or three, there wouldn't have been any problem, I could have taken measures, I would have known what to do. But now the waiting was losing all form, for every day that incompetent administrator would promise me: Tomorrow, perhaps, or surely the day after tomorrow. Only the weekends gave rhythm to this infernal idleness, for on weekends offices are closed. And so I was fading away; the longer the wait, the more my substance slowly dissolved. I was having more and more trouble sleeping; at night, impossible to fall asleep; I was reduced to taking pills, something I'd never done before. And in the morning, impossible to get up, a black, crushing fatigue nailed me to the bed, sometimes till afternoon; often, I finally got up for just a few hours, before falling back asleep, exhausted, until dinner. Then insomnia would reclaim its rights.

Irritation overwhelmed my thinking and my senses; irregularity ruled over me. I drank, but even that had no consistency. When I had a bottle, I would empty it with frightening swiftness; but once it was empty, I wouldn't buy another for days and days. I still wanted to drink, I desired it terribly, but to go out to buy another bottle was beyond me. As an excuse I dreamed up money problems, but that was just a vain pretext, good enough, though, for my paralysis. And during this time, other desires, even more ambiguous, hollowed out my body through and through. I didn't try to satisfy them directly; but alone in my room, I toyed with them, sometimes until I drew blood.

Once, already, I had found myself in a similar state. It was certainly during another wait. But back then I was even more lost, at least I think I can say that now. In any case, either because I had more strength then, or, on the contrary, because my weakness stripped away all my defenses, I had taken things much further. This is how I had found myself one night along the city's embankments, roaming the area where you can always run into a few suffering souls, greedy for some other whose inner emptiness could fulfill their own for a few hours, fill them with emptiness (it's one way to see things; there are others). It was certainly a disreputable place, which after a certain time of night fell under the jurisdiction of the vice squad. Playing hard to get, in my despair, I let a few walk by; my choice, almost at random, finally fell on a young black man. I think I can say he was a nice boy; he was in any case very shy. We walked for a long time, we didn't even touch until we reached his place. He didn't really know what to do, I had to guide him. But he gave in readily enough to my demands. Thus I submitted my body to his, for hours. Shame, pain, nothing was enough, I was nothing more than my emptiness, and the more I thrust that young man into it, the more I let myself be invaded by his frame, his musculature, his thick but strangely pointy cock, the more this emptiness opened up, deepened, and revealed to me the gloomy reaches of its immensity. In the end, it was the flesh that weakened, stumbled. The boy, sinking into an ordinary confusion, already thought he was in love. The cold took over me, his gushing disgusted me, I disgusted myself even more. I got dressed and went out, cutting short his declarations. On the landing of his wretched room stood the toilet, but I was in too much of a hurry, too crushed with shame, I didn't stop. This was a mistake, for an irresistible need seized me a few moments later, in the street. It wasn't yet dawn, all the cafés on my way were closed. Somehow I reached the building where I lived. I had to use the service entrance; by a miracle, I found a toilet on the ground floor—I couldn't take it any longer. Red, breathless with anguish, I rushed into it without even closing the door, almost too late, I let everything go. It was very unpleasant, believe me. My guts tied into knots, I stayed for a long time glued to this can, jumping at the slightest sound, terrified someone would discover me. I was sweating, there was shit everywhere. I managed to clean my pants and the edge of the toilet seat; as for my underpants, I didn't even try, I extricated myself from them and threw them in one of the garbage cans in the courtyard, burying them beneath the trash. Trembling, emptied out, I went up to my room. So much filth suffocated me, but at the same time I desired more, I desired madly to sink into it, I lost all notion of myself, my body was overcome with madness; contorted, I was illuminated by so much horror, I wanted to start again and never stop. Sleep calmed me down a little. Some time later…but let's drop this silliness, that's enough. At the time, then, that I started out talking about, I certainly hadn't gone this far, except perhaps in dreams. The way, though, seemed very much the same. But my situation featured a few differences, probably they played their part as well. First of all, I had an aim, a specific destination, which hadn't always been the case. What's more, I had someone to write to. Of course, her absence, her distance didn't improve my low spirits any. But the role of this distance in the ravings of my mind would be far more complex to define. Perhaps it contributed as well; but on the other hand, it seems to me that it might have been an attenuating factor, inasmuch as it offered my unhealthy avidity an outlet—fictive perhaps, but undeniably effective—an outlet, then, that took the form of exorbitantly expensive phone calls and especially a series of endless letters, written sometimes over the space of several days. Curiously, these letters and these calls, if they weren't entirely devoid of a certain eroticism, remained on the whole quite chaste, and sometimes even took on a quasi-idealistic turn. Given the state I was in, this may seem strange, all the more so since, as I have said, it worked out well, in a way, for my desires. Not that there was any sort of sublimation involved, far from it. In fact, the most tender words could bring a rush of lewd images into my head, some indeed concerning my correspondent, but others, rather, figures such as the boy I had once picked up by the river. Similarly, after days that were almost calm and serene, I might end up writing horribly tormented, violent, despairing letters. In truth, all that made me and still makes me dizzy. Still, the fact remains that in this way time went by. It's true, it went by, somehow. But it was very trying. It must be said: one day, the wait came to an end. But you can be sure it will start again.

– WINTER 1996

Between Planes

My misfortune is that there had been this contact, that a part of me had remained caught by her and had gotten me tangled up in the workings of this machine. Without that, nothing would have happened, I could have admired her, desired her calmly, and her indifference would never have touched me. It had begun during a brief visit to K—. I had met an old friend there, A., who had put me up at her place, on her sofa. C., who shared the apartment with A., had come back at four in the morning (the train, apparently, had gotten stuck), making a huge racket because she thought the door was locked, and had left again at six. During the day, I had come across her at A.'s office, overexcited, always in motion, a manic whirlwind that left no room for getting acquainted. She seemed unable to stop even for an instant. Her features were hard, but mobile, and not without beauty; and especially she had a furious energy, concentrated on work to the exclusion of all else, but capable too at times of generating bursts of lively cheerfulness that lit up those who otherwise just kept bouncing off of her or bumping against her. A. had already left, leaving me in the apartment. I would probably not have seen much of C., since I myself was supposed to leave the next day; that morning, there were riots in the city, all flights were suspended, and we stayed stuck in the apartment. In the afternoon, unable to bear it any more, C. decided to go out, and I offered to go with her; the authorities, because of the situation, had forbidden the use of vehicles; adhering to the letter if not the spirit of their instructions, we went out on foot. At the time I had a slight injury on my big toe, an injury that due to the climate and the irregularity of my way of life had degenerated into a nasty infection. So I was limping, and our journey across the city was a comic spectacle—she straight, proud, hurried, and I hobbling along, more than a little amused by the situation. Our shopping done with, as all work was out of the question for that day, we sat on the terrace of a bar on the main street for a beer. This was the first time since she had arrived in K—, she told me, that she had taken such a break. We chatted, she told me about her many trips, her stays in countries where I myself had long dreamed of going. An old comrade, whom I hadn't seen in a year, joined us, just as surprised as us by this unexpected day off, and we traded a few memories of the country where we had met, an atrocious region, but one that had seduced us both. The beer was cold, the terrace sunny, the rioters passed by in commandeered trucks, waving green branches and chanting slogans against the new authorities. It was pleasant, I think I can say that even C. had relaxed a little, and we were both in a cheerful mood when we returned to the apartment. The state of my foot had grown worse, and it had become very painful to walk. C. offered to cut open the abscess a little in order to relieve it. I had had a few drinks, and I agreed. I settled into an armchair and lit a cigar as she set to work, my foot wedged between her thighs. Her colleague D., exhausted, had fallen asleep sitting on the sofa, and the wild laughter that the pain of the operation strangely caused me didn't awaken her. Between fits of laughter I dragged furiously on my cigar, C. kept making me drink and scraping away at the infection; I took such a keen pleasure in this charming operation that I hardly noticed the discomfort. I put an end to it when I reached the end of my cigar. C. held my foot very tenderly, she cleaned it and bandaged it properly; D., waking, went to bed. C. and I, I think, stayed talking for a long time. Our hands sought each other, touched, played with each other, intertwined. We were still drinking, nothing else happened, the damage had already been done.

The next morning I found C. in her usual frenzy. She was leaving on a mission to the other side of the country; having already lost twenty-four hours, her natural impatience had been exacerbated, and the office resounded with her orders and her movements. I found her sitting down for a minute, thinking, and I took her hand; she was smiling, and mechanically stroked my palm. I had to leave, she was running down a hallway, also in a hurry: she kissed me quickly on the mouth and disappeared.

The airport was a complete mess. Six huge military cargo planes had landed one after the other, no one could point mine out to me; I limped furiously from one to the other, grinding my teeth in pain as the sun beat down on me, winding my way between the sacks of food and the crates of supplies being unloaded, the pickup trucks weaving across the tarmac, the furious soldiers, the lines of haggard people waited to be evacuated, I called out in Russian to the Ukrainian or Lithuanian pilots to ask their destination, they themselves often weren't sure. I actually came close to getting on the wrong plane and landing in the wrong country. I found C. under the wing of an Endover, crouching down with two colleagues, making plans and issuing last-minute instructions. She greeted me distractedly, everything was so confused that I didn't pay much attention to it. I climbed into the Endover; she was taking one of the big cargo planes heading west.

I had counted on seeing her the following week; but it would be over a month. The day before my return to K—, a doctor friend examined my foot and formally forbade me to travel. I was dismayed, but there was nothing to be done: the infection was far advanced, it was threatening the bone, I needed surgery right away. The country where we were didn't have adequate infrastructure; he advised me to go to the capital of a nearby country, where there was an excellent hospital. Appalled by the idea of not being able to join C. again, I had to resign myself to it. In K—, C.'s favorite perfume had disappeared; a friend had quickly shipped me a bottle; unable to go offer it to her in person, I packed it up and, before my departure, asked her office to forward it to where she was. I added a magnificent card, a Vermeer showing a girl sitting at a table in front of a window, her face in full light, holding a glass and smiling at a proud soldier shown from behind. I found this girl's face luminous, and I wrote a brief message on the back of the card: I tried for a charming, ironic tone, I don't know, maybe I succeeded. I was too unsure of what was happening really to express what was overwhelming me, but I also didn't want to seem cold, indifferent, as my letters so often are, incapable of expressing true emotions. Still in doubt, I sealed the card and handed it and the perfume over to a colleague of C.'s, who promised me they'd be forwarded.

He would not keep his promise; but then nothing would happen as planned. C. in fact still hadn't returned to K—: this news, which had wrenched my heart when I learned it, consoled me a little now for my forced departure, and I hoped that my return from convalescence would coincide with hers. Such was not to be the case, of course. The Fates, those teases, reveled in scrambling up our movements. The operation went very well, my surgeon turned out to be an old and admirably eccentric German, who livened up the procedure by holding forth, as he cut away at me, on the history of the medical use of cocaine from 1875 to the present. I thus learned that the invention of cocaine derivatives, preserving the anesthetic properties of the product while suppressing its euphoric aspects, had been stimulated by the excessive love the greatest doctors and surgeons of the time had for this drug, a love that motivated them to empty their shelves of it in order to consume it through the nose, the veins, and even, at that time, through the eyes. This problem, quite embarrassing for the reputation of the medical profession, came to an end in 1919 with the appearance of Novocain, a distant and coarse ancestor of the miraculous molecule that now made it possible that only the unpleasant scraping sound of the scalpel carving through my flesh distracted me from the surgeon's eloquence. I had to keep to my bed for a few days; once I was, precariously and painfully, on my feet again, I inquired about departing flights. I was booked on a Friday flight for G——, the city where most of the flights leaving for K—— originated. I had a lot of work to catch up on elsewhere, but I wasn't worried about taking the not very professional liberty of adjusting my travel plans this way. I called K——: C. was neither there, nor even in the city in the West where she had stayed to work (the city of M——), but had returned to G—— to report on her activities. I was delighted: I could, without any qualms, spend the weekend in her company in G——, then see to my affairs elsewhere and join her again later on. Then the people who controlled the airplanes canceled my booking: there was freight, they explained, that was more important. There were no planes before Monday, I was in despair, I knew that C. would have gone back to M—— by then. For some time now, I realized, this woman had completely occupied my life, and at bottom I even delighted at the suffering that the impossibility of seeing her again caused me, so strong was the emotion. I decided to call her in G—— (I was very anxious about how she would welcome such an importunate step): she seemed delighted to hear from me; her voice pierced my soul. She was leaving Saturday for K——, then from there for M——. I asked her to wait for me before going to K——, she couldn't, but promised to meet me again a little later. "See you soon, dear child," she said as she hung up; torn between the pleasure these words gave me and the frustration of not being able to see her again, I spent the afternoon trying every way possible to find a plane. Another organization had chartered one, I contacted a friend there, he promised to find me a seat on it; two hours later, he called me back to explain that his boss had vetoed it (I learned later on that another woman, whom I only barely knew, but who for a reason I never found out heartily detested me, had struck my name from the list). I thus spent several hours oscillating between the most violent hope and the blackest rage. I stormed, limping from one office to the other, I drove the secretaries mad with my obstinacy, I forced them to chase down leads whose uselessness was obvious, but which made them lose their time and their patience. At six in the evening, a miracle occurred: the first carrier, whom I had called back as a last resort, calmly informed me that he not only had room for me, but also for some two hundred kilos of freight that I was supposed to bring back. This was a call to action, since of course the freight wasn't ready, the customs papers were missing, the freight forwarder was closed for the day: by eight o'clock, though, everything was in order. I had to be at the airport at six in the morning, I was there at 5:30, it didn't open till 6:30, and at 7:00 they came to tell me that the plane had broken down and wouldn't fly that day. My despondency was so profound that I was only barely aware of the appalling comedy of the situation. In the afternoon I called C. again: she was still leaving the next day and couldn't delay her trip, but hearing her comforted me a little. I did indeed leave the next day. The plane was flying on to the city where I was supposed to work, there was no point for me to get out at G —, now that C. was no longer there. On the flight, I devised the mad hope of meeting her for a few minutes on the tarmac in G —, of being able to speak to her even if only for a moment, see her eyes and her smile, kiss her. Her plane, of course, had left hours earlier.

I spent a week working with my colleagues, and I planned then on returning to K — : I had in fact to settle some debts there, which justified a trip that my sense of duty would not otherwise have permitted. I had to go back through G——, the planes for K—— were canceled several days in a row; but C. was still in M——, so I was patient. C.'s superior then told me that she was supposed to return to K—— on Wednesday, the day of my own departure. I was happy, but terrified at the idea of another unforeseen occurrence. The plane I was supposed to take would fly on from K—— to M—— and then return to K——; before I learned she would be on the return trip, I had decided to make this additional journey and bring her a flower, even if only to see her for half an hour. So I modified this plan somewhat: I would get off at K——, but would still send her the flower, without telling her from whom it came, to greet her in the plane. The spitefulness of an office manager, who also seemed to hate me, nearly made me miss this plane: whereas I had booked my seat days before, my name didn't appear on the list, and the employee in charge of boarding refused to let me get on. I must have looked quite a sight in my wretchedness, standing on the tarmac holding a big yellow flower, so incongruous in this context that I hesitated for a long time before daring to take it with me. But a friend showed up at the right moment, one who supervised the flights directly, and he put me on the plane. On board there was a Swede who was continuing on to M——: I gave him the flower, with precise instructions. The flight was horrible, we were caught for half an hour in a violent storm; I reassured myself by telling myself that such bumps must be normal for such a small plane, but when we arrived in K——, I saw that the pilots were livid. I soon came across C.'s superior, with whom I was developing a strong camaraderie; C. was supposed to arrive a few hours later.

I found her that afternoon in the offices, amazed that there hadn't been any additional mishaps, that she hadn't, for instance, returned to G— without stopping in K—. "So, you didn't want to make the round trip to accompany me," she scolded. "Ah, but I sent you a flower in my place." She hadn't received it, the Swede had forgotten it on the plane. She had seen it when boarding and wondered who it could be for, where it could have come from. Even for that, I was happy of the gesture. As for the perfume, she told me later, it had never been sent on to M—, but she had picked it up during her trip to G—, and it had made her very happy, these last few weeks, to be able thus to fight the abominable stench of the people she had to take care of.

She had kissed me in a friendly way when I arrived; everything, from that moment on, would become more difficult. I said so earlier, I had gone too far forward, I had too hurriedly opened a door that my instincts, in general quite good, usually kept firmly closed.

Her withdrawal, from that moment on, slowly tore me apart. In the days that followed, she remained immersed in her frantic activities; from time to time, she granted me a moment of conversation, but right away some work-related thought would distract her and she would set off again. She was at the end of her contract and was about to leave the country; she had received several offers, one, from her present employer, involving the city where I was usually posted (but that didn't interest her at all), another to return to M— for a different organization, and still others for different countries.

She couldn't make up her mind, she discussed it with every-one, and also carried on endlessly about all the problems she had encountered in M—. At the time, wounded by her indifference, I thought I had been terribly mistaken, that I had radically misinterpreted signs that for her must have been only those of friendship; later on, I came to think that her time in M—, which had visibly exhausted her, must have touched a certain point in such a way that she, who always seemed so sure of what she was doing and of where she was going, had in fact completely lost her bearings, and now could only focus on her concrete problems, an ultimate ref-uge. She remained friendly; but whatever the reason, she had shifted away from the brief contact that had formed between us, and this disengagement quickly broke me apart. The hardest thing was the nights: she invited me to stay with her, she refused to let me sleep on the couch, she insisted on putting me in her room, in a separate bed. Thus, she slept a meter away from me, almost naked, and it was impossible for me to touch her. I myself was exhausted by my work of the last few months, by my disgust with the country in which I was working, by my nagging uncertainty about the usefulness of the actions I was organizing; the indifference of C., or simply her absence, finished plunging me into misery. I always drink a lot, I drank even more. I almost didn't sleep, and every night, as I went to bed with this separation between our bodies, I felt as if I were skewering myself on a knife. I would wake up with a start, sometimes went back to sleep; in the morning, I was emptied out, exhausted, and the extremely unpleasant matters I had come to settle in K— only added to my disarray. Once my eyes were used to the darkness, at night, I could clearly see her shape; sometimes her sheet slid off, and I would gaze for a long time at her white back, her sharp little breasts. Rarely have I felt a more violent yet less physical desire: what my body sought wasn't so much to make love with her as simply to press itself against her. I was distraught, in an extreme state, I was losing my grip; when we spoke, my conversation was often flat, tense, and it was impossible for me to express what was gnawing away at me. She too was a little ill and wasn't sleeping well. Thus strange moments would occur that I still don't understand. Once, I remember, caught in our respective insomnias, our eyes met, and we looked at each other for a long time, without smiling, without speaking. Another time, in a similar moment, where the loss of sleep seemed to make her suffer almost as much as me, I held my hand out from one bed to the other, and she took it until she fell back asleep. The last night of our stay in K—, she had gone to bed before me, I sat on the edge of my bed, facing her, and took her hand; overwhelmed with fatigue and sadness, I kissed that hand, I caressed it, and finally placed my head on it for a long while. I don't know if we spoke, or if I simply surrendered to that hand. She finally took it back. Mad with suffering, almost in tears, I leaned over her and kissed her on the lips, gently. Then I went to bed. That night was as bad as the others. I can't manage to grasp the significance of these moments when, if she wasn't encouraging me at all, she certainly wasn't pushing me away either. But something very strong prevented me from pushing, from provoking her to a rejection that would at least have had the merit of being clear. Perhaps she herself was in a form of despair that floated along next to mine without being able to meet it. In our conversations, she certainly didn't imply this: she spoke only about the positive aspects of her life, or else about her concrete problems, which corresponded to her aggressive, determined character. She had a child, I haven't mentioned that, she wanted to see him again and spoke to me passionately about him. As for her husband, he had vanished from the picture some time ago. I suspect something must have been eating away at her, something fundamental that pushed her among other things to live such an unstable life, but she must have been incapable, by her very nature, of recognizing it. That must be the great difference between us. On the last day, as I was watching her pack, she asked me some questions about me. I could only answer superficially: it seemed impossible, from her questions and her tone, for her to understand or accept true answers, even if I had been capable of formulating them. "Are you suffering?" she asked me point-blank; once again, I evaded the question. The conversation didn't go much further and left me confused. I didn't know if I had said too much or too little. Her reaction was illegible, once again she was elsewhere, caught up in her departure. We were all taking, along with her colleague D., a commercial flight for G——. She didn't want to stop in G—— but was forced to for administrative reasons. The boarding, at the airport, was extremely chaotic, but the flight was quick. I had hoped to take a room in the same hotel as she: one last chance, I said to myself, to resolve this story one way or another. Then, on the plane, as she was chatting away with D., despair over-whelmed me completely, I felt soiled, and I was overcome with the desire to just drop the whole thing, to leave her at the airport in G — and never to see her again, never to expose myself again to this indifference whose profound ambiguity was tearing me apart. My weakness got the upper hand, I went to that hotel: there were no more rooms. Good, I said to myself, at least that's settled for me. We agreed to meet at eight that evening; I came, but she wasn't there anymore. She had left a note at the reception for another man, whom she had to see for professional reasons: for me, nothing. Later that evening, I found her in a restaurant with all her colleagues. She was immersed in conversation with her boss, she barely looked at me. Taking advantage of a pause, I made a date with her for the next afternoon, for lunch. She offhandedly agreed and told me to come find her at the office. They all left soon afterwards and she barely said goodbye to me. She was far, very far away. The next day, around noon, I found her at the office with D., settling their administrative problems. She was exasperated and paid almost no attention to my presence. I waited for an hour, asking her two or three times if she planned on lunching with me: "I don't know, I don't know," she replied, "I have to go back to the hotel." I was sitting in the lobby of the office where she was with the administrator when a little black and white bird flew in. It began walking around with disjointed but calm steps, surprised at the closed door. Then it turned on a little moth that was sleeping there and attacked it with its beak. The moth struggled, but in vain, and the bird swallowed it in a cloud of scales, a fine white dust of torn off wings forming a luminous halo around its head. C. was chatting with D., they were waiting for the administrator to pay them, they were talking animatedly about incidents of their work, laughing. I sat down near them, useless. Then the administrator returned. Once again, I asked C. if she wanted to come have lunch: her answer remained vague, it was obvious that her problems had completely absorbed her, I was only disturbing her. I left with barely a word, she did nothing to hold me back. The next day, the flight that was supposed to carry me away from there was canceled because of a holiday.

– SPRING 1997

Fait Accompli

So there she had said that and already it was irreparable. For him as well as for her not being the kind of man to take that lightly. But making a decision right away was not something he was capable of, nor she. So first think, then talk. But even before thinking first not thinking, waiting, letting a little time pass, foul time, in any case there would be enough left, even if in this precise case it was objectively limited, for concrete physiological reasons making it so that a certain amount of time of no reflection and of no discussion and hence of no decision would in itself be a decision, a decision made. So not to think right away, so as not to think in the heat of the moment, but still to think, and fairly quickly, when the moment is lukewarm rather than cold. So she then on her side first not thinking and then rather quickly thinking, and he on his side as well. The other just growing. He then thinking but without knowing how she was thinking, telling himself that in any case for him it was of no importance how she thought since she is the one who did the thing, so she has only to wait, and if no decision then in fact decision, thus it's up to him to think now. First error of reasoning perhaps but nonetheless that is how he proceeds. For him, then, two questions, that is question 1 the other or not the other, and question 2 her or not her. To these two questions four solutions, that is solution 1 him without her without the other, solution 2 him with her without the other, solution 3 him without her with the other, solution 4 him with her with the other. Now for him at this stage with the other out of the question and hence out of the question solutions 3 and 4, remain thus numbers 1 or 2, without the other with or without her, hence why not with, it wasn't so bad, and it would be almost like before, except that in the meantime there would have been that. But here precisely there is a problem, since if for him with the other out of the question, for her without the other out of the question, of this he is certain, even without asking, her I mean. So if for her without the other out of the question, then out of the question solutions 1 and 2, remain thus numbers 3 and 4, already out of the question. So let's start again. For him solution 4 absolutely out of the question since the chains the locked door the key thrown in the river. Solution 1 out of the question as well since for him no advantage and for her absolutely out of the question. Solution 2 given the facts and with things as they are almost ideal for him but for her the opposite. And what's more devilishly problematic since even if he could cajole her into it through a skillful combination of feelings and blackmail there would always be that and the weight and the fault of that, a fault which given that it would be he who would have cajoled her into this solution would fall automatically on him, whether she wanted it or not, whether she said so or not, and thus it would not at all be like before, since even if there were no more other which after all would be a great relief there would be that over him and thus also in another manner the cage the locked window the key thrown in the pond, and fault and suffering as well. Thus remains solution 3, ideal neither for him since no more her nor for her since no more him, but conceivable all the same since for her the other so not that, and for him since no more her not really the other either, since the other remains with her, that goes without saying, so even if in a certain manner the other in any case not the bars the iron door the key hanging on its nail and not that either so neither fault nor suffering, except the suffering of no more her nonetheless in the long run bearable especially given the other options, likewise for her in the long run also if not right away. A solution, then, if not perfect, in any case the least worst, given the situation, hence almost elegant in its own way, given the dilemma, more in any case than solution 2, solution less worse for him as has been said, but certainly more worse for her, and no doubt more more worse for her than it would be more less worse for him, if one could measure this sort of gradation of worstness with any precision that is certainly what one would judge, hence the conclusion that solution 3 the least worst absolutely, solutions 1 and 4 being regarded as out of the question, solution 1 for her as well as for him, solution 4 for him absolutely even if for her the ideal solution henceforth known as the eating one's cake and having it too solution. This being settled time to talk since by dint of not thinking and then thinking time is passing, foul time, and the other is growing, the foul other, isn't he, and by the way why not the foul other, isn't she, after all there's no way to know, yet precisely in this case the French language with the full weight of its history settles the matter, without asking anyone's opinion, when in doubt as in the case of mixed plurals, thus the other he and not she, a little arbitrary perhaps, but that's the way it is, blame the French language, in English one would just write *it*. Talking, then, a conversation in short, like many others. Yet a conversation means a scene, no escaping convention. The conversation thus takes place in a small park, by the side of a grey pond, in the clatter of buses and trolleys passing close by, between two rows of trees among which are chestnut trees, recognizable by their eggplant-shaped leaves and especially by the chestnuts strewing the ground. It's fall and the yellowing leaves on the trees including on the chestnut trees are falling and strewing the ground and floating on the grey water of the pond and are sent whirling by the buses and the trolleys passing close by, and as for them their sad footsteps tread on the yellow and brown leaves and a few rare chestnuts and many husks, the green ones freshly fallen and the brown ones yesterday's or the day before yesterday's, shaken from the chestnut branches by filthy brats who collect the chestnuts for their slingshots, hence rare, but leave the husks, hence many. No that won't do. Let's say then instead a subway station, for instance, at random, the Mayakovskaya station in the Moscow subway, with all along its vaulted ceiling pretty oval mosaics, planes, blimps, parachutists, young athletes bursting with Soviet health and joy, all the way down the long hall with at the very end the bust of the poet, the foul bust, the foul poet. They are walking, she with her ashamed and suffering eyes fixed on the concrete of the platform, he with his face raised to the mosaics, the fragments of colors planted between the arches, all this imaginary innocence. No that won't do either. In fact they are sitting since thinking about this has tired them too much to walk. In a park at night on a bench with all around them bawling drunkards, or else in a restaurant next to a bluish-green aquarium, or both at once, that is from the park to the restaurant to flee the drunkards then after the meal from the restaurant to the park, what in fact do these scenic details matter, the main thing is that they are seated and talking, or else they are seated and silent, or else they are walking and talking, or else they are walking and silent, or else he is walking back and forth and is silent and she is seated and with her ashamed and suffering eyes fixed on the table is also silent, or else he is the one seated and who with his face raised to the ceiling is silent, and she who is pacing back and forth and is also silent, the same when talking, he walking she seated, or she walking and he seated. Or else another variant they write letters that they hand each other or else that they leave on a table saying There, I've written, read. The main thing is that they are communicating, having done with not thinking and then thinking, except when they are not communicating, but given the situation even this non-communication is one, communication I mean. The other it should be said in passing as they are discussing it or not discussing it is living its other life, five millimeters and the heart systole diastole, probably six millimeters by the time they're done discussing it, they should hurry. So he explains to her the questions 1 and 2 and the solutions 1 2 3 and 4, number 1 presenting no interest either for her nor for him and number 4 out of the question for the reasons already stated, thus remain number 2 and number 3, yet number 2 means that and the weight and the fault of that which would not fail no matter what she says to come weigh on his shoulders, hence number 3, the least worst solution, but there surprise, since for her number 3 out of the question, if no him then no other, no other without him, that's the way it is, thus if number 3 then that and thus number 3 is in fact number 1, no other and her without him, him without her and without the other, shit, that screws everything up, let's start again. So if number 3 out of the question for her to the point of being the same as number 1, his 3 leading automatically as it were to her 1, and number 4 known as far as she is concerned as eating one's cake and having it too out of the question for him since the cage the ball and chain the key thrown down the well, there remains number 2 which for the record is him with her without the other so then that, and quickly, it's growing. But that for her horror the garbage can her on all fours and blood on the floor, no, and what's more if him with her why not the other, what's the difference, impertinent woman's logic. So he explains to her the cell the locked door, she understands but the other in green fields rivers what's to be done. No fields no rivers for the other for the other the vacuum cleaner and blood on the floor, or else yes the fields the river, but without him, solution 3 for the record, but no since if no him then no other, solution 1, on all fours the matchbox the blood on the floor, and what's more no him, absolute woe. Remains thus number 4 known as for the record eating one's cake and having it too. This now called a conversation. Hard under such conditions to make any progress since he having carefully analyzed it all the solutions 1 2

3 and 4 to the questions 1 and 2, elementary logic, would be fully disposed to draw the necessary conclusions, yet when he talks to her about him she talks to him about the other and when he talks to her about the other she talks to him about him, thus transforming solution 3 into solution 1 and solution 2 into solution 4, the one known as eating one's cake and having it too, for the record even if we are repeating ourselves a bit. So she then asking him to explain once again why number 4 out of the question, why him and the other together impossible, and he explaining to her once again the bars on the window the door triple locked the key thrown in the middle of the Atlantic, and she saying But no the green fields the rivers, and he replying I don't give a fuck about your fields and your rivers, that's not the problem, the problem is the horror, and they thus realizing that already at bottom they couldn't agree, for at bottom she still had hope, foul hope, that's a quotation you will have noticed, that it would be less bad than it had been before, that toward less worse they would head and the other too, and that as bad as it might be for the other bad would always be less bad than that, the worst would be less worse than nothing, vile optimism since he for one remained firmly convinced that bad it had been and worse it would yet be, and probably even worse beyond the worst imaginable, for imagination has its limits, but the worst does not, and that this other would once again be a story of rats in a cage, shit, another quotation, enough quotations, let us resume. Thus, the horror being a given, no need to shovel more on, no need to send yet another one to the slaughter, to perpetuate thus the horror forever and ever, better to call it a day here and now. But here and now is

precisely where the other is, yes, that he had understood quite well, thank you, and thus for the other not to be here and now one had to go through that, yes, that too he had understood quite well, thank you, but for him that was less worse than the cage and the key and also the rats and the slaughter for the poor mindless other with its systoles diastoles, so there you go, solution 2, but not for her, for her number 2 was the garbage can her on all fours and the other in the matchbox and the blood everywhere everywhere everywhere, all right, so let's take it from the top, solution 3, no garbage can no her on all fours and also no cage and no key, the fields yes, everything, except him far away from all that, solution as one can see if not ideal in any case the least worst since cutting everyone's losses, for her no blood, for him no bars, for the other rivers, only problem she won't have it, no him then no other, that's the way it is, stubborn bitch, goddamn it. Let's start again. Now what does she want she wants eating one's cake and having it too that is for the record solution 4, but that is out of the question and there is no way she can force it on him, inasmuch as small reminder the fault is hers, if there is the other when there shouldn't have been one it's because there was a fault, and the fault is hers and hers only, on this point everyone is in agreement, she didn't do it on purpose but still there was a mistake and from the mistake the other, thus a fault, hers and hers only, that's settled, let's move on. The fault given there remain four solutions, that is number 1 number 2 number 3 and number 4 already defined above reread if you don't remember, now number 1 being of no interest to anyone and number 4 known as eating one's cake and having it too being out of the question for him, there remain in all good logic and we are nothing if not logical number 2 and number 3. Yet she as soon as he talks to her of the other talks to him of him and thus passes from number 3 to number 2 and as soon as he talks to her of her talks to him of the other thus passing from number 2 to number 4, which is cunning but he says no and there they go again. Solution 3 she won't have if number 3 then number 1 the basin the blood and what's more no him. Remains number 2 but number 2 is also that, is also the vacuum cleaner the basin the blood on the floor me on all fours my love in the garbage can my love in the matchbox the horror a situation that you will have certainly noted all sentimental questions set aside would also have the effect of transferring the fault from her to him, as indicated above, reread if you've forgotten, for the initial fault is hers everyone agrees on that but given the fault there is solution 4 known as eating one's cake and having it too, and if not number 4 then number 2 with the matchbox on all fours, we'll come back to that, number 3 out of the question for she won't have it if number 3 then number 1, yes but he won't have number 4, ah but that's not the same thing oh well okay then, back to number 2, the basin the blood and all that she is willing, she says yes to the basin, but there's nothing to be done, the fault passes to him, since fault there is since for her that means her on all fours and the blood, the horror, yes but the other for him is also the horror, the cage and the walls and the rats, ah but that's not quite the same thing oh well okay then, it's in your head and the matchbox that's not in your head yes you are right I will do it then solution 2 but you must know the horror ah yes the horror and thus the fault displaced the fault mine originally but given will become your fault as a consequence and worse still since not yet given since not mandatory since there is choice since there exists another solution solution 4 as you call it known as eating your cake and having it too but I understand that you rule it out yes I understand the cage and all that yes I understand and the fault is mine thus solution 2 as you call it since not number 3 as you call it since all alone I couldn't all alone it will also be that so from the moment that you rule out number 4 known as eating your cake and having it too as you call it it will be that the garbage can love in the garbage can blood everywhere but I will do it and I won't blame you darling there will be no fault on you darling you just have to be sure, sure of the locked room and the key thrown down the sewer, sure of the rats in a cage and I know the quotation, sure also that something will be worse than nothing, sure of all that since if you are sure then it will be that the vacuum cleaner darling and our love in the garbage can darling and me your love on all fours in the blood trying to put back my love darling in a matchbox in me darling in my empty body so you have to be sure, sure of your call, if you aren't there remains solution 4 known as eating your cake and having it too as you call it.

– FALL 2002

Story about Nothing

It was only the other day this story came to my mind. I was driving down the northern highway; the sun, a ball of fire boring a hole into the pale sky, was crushing everything with its light and heat, and, overcome with torpor beneath this vast summer sky, I was floating unawares on the verge of sleep. I didn't know where I was going; to tell the truth, I didn't really know if I was driving, or if, stretched out in this vast heat on the sheetless rectangle of my mattress, I was dreaming that I was driving, or even if I was having this sleeping-driver dream in the midst of driving, my hands inert on the black leather hoop of the steering wheel. Sleeping, I said to myself: one should write about this and about nothing else, not about people, not about me, not about absence or about presence, not about life or about death, not about things seen or heard, not about love, not about time. Already, it had taken shape. Obeying a sign shaped like a triangle, I left the highway and headed for the sea. Parking lots followed one another, monotonous, crowded with cars baking in the sun. Finally I noticed an out-of-the-way trail and took it. It led to a little stretch of beach, none too clean, but almost empty: only a few people had spread out the colored squares of their towels and were lazing about, naked and ruddy, exposed to the rage of the sun or else half-hidden under the laughable disks of little parasols. This suited me, and I too undressed and went into the water. It was warm and soft, and instead of waking me up, this monotonous, lapping expanse, swollen with a huge repetitious murmur, lulled me to sleep even more, enveloping my dormant body in the sinuous play of its forms and sounds. Naked, I floated on my back, my head borne by the waves, my eyes blind beneath the triumphant sky, pierced at its zenith by the bleak insatiable fire of the sun, and I dreamed I was swimming out to sea, calmly, with patience and rhythm, pitting without exhausting it the strength of my muscles against the inertia of this immense, shapeless, sly mass agitated by a placid, continuous violence; from time to time, my head went under water, and, with eyes closed against the biting salt, I lost all notion of space, I found myself tossed about, overcome, a dull anguish weighing down my limbs that seemed to move like seaweed, with no more force or power, each limb separate from the others and incapable of rediscovering a whole that might have served to give sense and direction to this movement; in my lungs, the air was turning sour, sucking in my ribs; then a contrary surge of the waves would hurl me back to the sky, my mouth open in a circle just above the waves, whipped by seaspray, and I resumed my regular movements, forcing my way through this endless waste. This lasted a long time, until I heard a voice, a young woman with a loud, tinkling laugh: "No, silly, you're not swimming, you're dreaming you're swimming. Do you even know how to swim?"—"Of course

I do," I wanted to protest: but I opened my eyes in vain, I saw no one.

That same day, it comes back to me now, some friends had suggested celebrating my birthday; but I couldn't remember the date, or even the sign under which I was born. I was made that way: neither sad nor merry, neither open nor private, curious about everything but not interested in anything; I knew many people, but wasn't attached to anyone. It was not my fault; the blame falls on those who had reared me, or on my depraved nature, or else on a blow to the head I got in the fog, one fall night, on a high, dark mountain.

Scarcely had I gotten back to town than I met an acquaintance. He was coming down a broad staircase at the end of an empty rectangular esplanade, his pale suit shone in the sun; to see him better, I shaded my eyes with my hand, and he burst out laughing, exposing between his garnet lips two rows of regular, gleaming little teeth, all the while holding out his hand and taking me by the shoulder: "You don't remember me? We've been friends for a long time, though." He began chatting with me casually, about everything and nothing. It was a little surprising: I thought he had been dead for years. "Not at all! Not so far as I know, at least." We lingered a while on these steps, talking some more; he still held my shoulder in a friendly grip, his eyes laughing. I laughed too and shook his hand, before heading home.

Opening the door, I saw myself in the mirror, a large round mirror leaning against the wall, reflecting the horizontal rectangle of the striped mattress, it too lying on the floor, and the vertical rectangle of the open door, red on the outside, white on the inside. In the mirror, the face framed by the jambs of this door was looking at me, smiling calmly; I found it somewhat beautiful, but of a vague, undefined, blurred beauty. Night was falling, I pressed the switch: light leapt out, harsh and bright, from a bare lightbulb hanging over the mattress, reflected in the round mirror too. I had bought this mirror, its glass all pockmarked and partially tarnished, from a second-hand dealer, and I liked it immensely. It must have had a defect that I hadn't noticed; as time passed, a crack stretched out mysteriously from one edge; then another fissure began to branch off from the first, forming a little V at the bottom of the mirror, just like a woman's pubis; finally, a long horizontal line came to cross this V. The mirror kept staring at me, impassive, a mute cyclops's glum eye. Sometimes I would lay the mirror flat on the mattress and crouch along its edge, leaning on my hands. Depending on the angle, I would then see my features surprisingly abstract and very far away, or else just the lightbulb hanging on the ceiling, or else nothing, nothing at all, as if I were gazing not at a mirror but at a gaping, luminous pit, slightly purplish, carved into my bed, into which I could have tumbled head-first, to disappear forever. Sometimes too, I would put on female underclothes—stockings, dainty black lace panties, a padded bra—at times with a thin clinging dress, at others not, and for a long time I would examine this beautiful feminine form, elegant, aristocratic, its musculature subtle and well-defined, its skin white, beneath which snaked thick veins swollen with blood, losing in this way in the image all notion of time and place, of my person or of my thoughts. That a few tawdry rags bought in a hurry at the supermarket were enough to make a woman, a real image of a woman—that is what filled me with wonder, it was a spell, pure magic. Nothing could come to disturb this happiness. One time, though, a curious thing happened: a child, in the corner of my bedroom, said softly but clearly: "You shouldn't be doing that." I didn't know who he was, or what he was doing there, but I replied kindly: "And why not?"—"I would prefer that you didn't do it." I gazed at him, smiling tenderly. In the mirror's disk, the gossamer lace followed the arched loins of the figure reflected there, plunged between its buttocks; lower down, another band circled its thigh. I was still looking at the blond child, motionless and stubborn in his corner, his fists clenched alongside his legs; finally, without taking my eyes off him, I slowly stretched my hand out to the switch, pressed it, and everything, child and feminine form, circles and rectangles, vanished into the dark.

I also liked to go out in the street like that, with this lace underwear beneath my clothes: it produced a strange sensation in me—light and floating, as if both sexes at once were strolling in my body through the city. Sitting with a cold drink at a café terrace on a public square, I would examine the women passing by, think about their clothes, as light and airy as my feelings, about what they were wearing underneath, lace or fine fabrics, which they often showed glimpses of: for them, these delicate layers on their bodies added nothing, took away nothing, they were women in all simplicity, naked or clothed, with or without artifice, even coarsely dressed, or dressed like men, they remained women; these pieces of fabric, so maddening to me, were as natural to them as their own skin, it was just the texture of their lives, a pleasant and caressing thing perhaps, but one they could do without: at the very most, sometimes, pleasure might seize them by the throat as they slowly removed these garments in front of a man's avid desire. As for me, they transformed me completely, they made me a free oscillation, around which my desires floated freely, coming to bear on everything and nothing, settling only to take off and settle on their opposite, before coming back or going elsewhere, and I no longer knew if I was man or woman, unless someone told me. This made me astonishingly mobile and I loved that. But it was also possible that this was all a dream, like that other dream in which I was trying to decipher notes I had made when I awoke from yet a third dream, a long wonderful story, just like this one. I could see the words, a few doodles hastily sketched out, I was trying to reconstruct this lost dream, which fled from me imperceptibly but steadily, like sand trickling from one cone of the hourglass to the other; it escaped me just as this story is escaping me. To tell the truth, I never really knew if I was asleep or awake, this too someone had to come and tell me. But reality was never lacking in people ready to determine it, however arbitrarily, like that friend, the one on the stairs who should have been dead, but who was shaking my shoulder, laughing: "Hey there, are you sleeping?" He sat down opposite me and ordered, drank, ordered another. "I have something for you," he said, "I know you, you're going to like it." He took out a disk from his pocket and put it on the round table. "What is it?"—"You'll see, you'll see."

Already he was getting up and walking off without paying; that made me glad, I was happy for him for his trust, his freedom, his lightness. The disk, silvery in a thin, transparent square case, remained on the table, I forgot it when I left; I'd only taken a few steps before the waitress caught me by the sleeve to give it back to me. She had a beautiful smile, brown, silky skin: she too wore her body with ease, as if it weren't a miracle.

I climbed back up into my tall square tower, suspended high above the city. Down below, behind the last buildings, grey, metallic, the sea stood like a long wall beneath the pale summer sky; when a big ship passed by, it looked almost as if it were flying slowly beyond the city. Many cranes, blue or green, crisscrossed the sky with their stalks; to the right, the round mass of a small mountain rose to hide the line of the sea. I turned my computer on and inserted the disk my friend had left me. It was a short pornographic movie, made not by professionals but evidently by the people in it, two men and a woman, along with a fourth, the one holding the camera, who was never shown. Of the two men, the first was still young, with a massive body and closely cropped hair; the other was already settling into a hairy layer of fat, and wore long, rather outdated sideburns joined to his moustache. The woman wore black stockings and a red mask, and her coarse body showed signs of age; when she lowered her head, her chin formed thick folds with her neck; but she had magnificent hair, black and heavy, tied back at the neck by a rubber band. The two men were caressing her body; then the younger one began to fuck her, while the other dragged his cock over her lips. She was groaning softly, full of her pleasure but also attentive to the scene. The relationships between the characters intrigued me: there must have been a husband involved, or at least a lover, that seemed to me unavoidable, for this was obviously no callgirl paid for the pleasure of the two men, on the contrary, it was the men who had been placed at the service of this woman's pleasure, yet something in their attitudes, especially in hers, passive in her pleasure, suggested that she had not organized the scene herself, but that it had been organized for her by another, who was thus sharing her pleasure. But who was it? The fat one with the sideburns, more open, less hurried in his gestures than the young one? Or the one holding the camera, whose lens remained focused on the body of the woman and what was happening to her? But one couldn't entirely rule out the possibility that the camera was held by another woman. Yet to these four actors had to be added a fifth, the main character of this little movie: the gaze. The entire spectacle had been staged with it in mind. There was of course the gaze of the man or woman holding the camera and studying the scene through his or her viewfinder, just as there was my own, contemplating it on my computer screen; but the gaze of the three naked figures on the green sheets was also put into play, redoubled not just by the expectation of the film to come, but also right then and there, by a large mirror that occupied the entire wall next to the bed, where they took turns observing themselves. At one point, a man—the fat one, or the one filming?—uttered a phrase in a language that I did not understand, Italian perhaps or some local dialect, and this phrase seemed to me to say:

"Do you like what you're seeing?" for the woman, still being fucked by the young one, was attentively watching herself being fucked and filmed in the big mirror. "Yes, yes," she panted; and the camera was no longer filming the three intertwined bodies, but just their reflection in the mirror, where the woman, sprawled in her pleasure, her eyes like black marbles in her red mask, gazed at herself panting, her mouth open, her tongue out like that of a bull exhausted by the matador's elusive red cloth, obscene and beautiful in her obscenity. She contemplated herself this way for a long time; then, slowly, she rolled her head over to the prick offered to her mouth. Afterwards, it went on, they moved her around, took turns penetrating her; and she, while giving in to their arms and bodies, to their greedy members, was also constantly observing herself in the mirror, as if to assure herself, Yes, that's really me, that sublime whore there, with the beautiful hair and this body that's so heavy and so female, being fucked by these two men, ah what happiness. The men too looked at themselves, but shiftily, snickering at times. It ended ritually, with their sperm on the woman's mouth, her face, her mask, her breasts, a brief orgasm frightfully meager after her own, which overflowed this little twenty-minute-long movie.

These images, so clumsy and ordinary, filled me with joy: transported into rapture, as if by the sweetness of a ripe peach, I felt as if I were about to lift off from the ground. Outside, now, it was dark; the city's lights shone in front of sky and sea confused into a single vast endless black surface. I watched the video several times; each time, it stuck in my gaze, nailed all my desires, usually so fluid, to a single blind point before which I found myself transfixed, breathless.

However, as I rather quickly discovered, this was just a poor sample of a considerable series, mass-produced by a production company a little savvier than the others; yet this knowledge changed nothing, absolutely nothing: these images remained what they were, frozen in the eternal repetition of their so violently human perfection. I no longer left my room, I hardly even moved from my mattress; I could just barely get up when I felt an urgent need. Eating, drinking, they no longer concerned me; of course I was ill, but I had no way of knowing that unless someone told me; but no one came, I stayed there alone in the midst of my funhouse mirrors, which altered not the image they reflected, but the very person who was mirrored. The same friend finally gave me, by telephone, some good advice: "You should go find a doctor." I had two doctors—thin, stiff women in their long white smocks, one still young and quite attractive, the other much older and more talkative too. "You definitely do not look well," she said with birdlike gestures. Together, they had me undress, listened to my chest, palpated me, examined the various orifices of my body, with comments that were cryptic to me, but no doubt rich in meaning for them. In the end, I found myself lying on my belly, with the older doctor, who had pulled on latex gloves, delicately parting the cleft of my buttocks, and the two women stood leaning over my anus as if over a well, calmly discoursing on what they saw there. They sent me home with some medicine, somewhat randomly selected I think, and I took it at random too, in the following spirit: if my condition got better, then the remedy was good, and if it got worse, then it was bad.

Despite my poor health, I still occasionally watched the little film. I had finally realized something: more than the sight of it, which had so absorbed me, it was the sound of this scene that moved me so violently. I made this discovery entirely by chance; by mistake, I had cut the sound on my computer; muted, these images were nothing more than grotesque gesticulations. Whereas all I had to do was close my eyes and listen to the groans, the gasps, the broken, stammered words, the interrupted breathing, to find myself rapt again: a dazzling, almost blinding discovery, this, but limited nonetheless, in that the echo of these sounds, which at first opened the way, itself ended up forming an elusive obstacle, flexible but insuperable; caught in its snare, I found myself once again rejected, brutally returned to myself, and thus everything began all over again, in a crazy whirling that only rooted me deeper in my own impossibility.

"Come with us!" my friend had called out, peremptorily—how to resist such a command? Thus I found myself with a whole company of people in another city, where a *feria* was taking place. Jubilation reigned in the streets, borne by a huge crowd, happy and overexcited, maddened as much by the liberties allowed on these few days as by the sun, the alcohol, the laughter, and the disordered jostling of bodies. We walked about aimlessly; whenever we felt like it, we would drink some chilled wine, standing in the street or packed into crowded cafés. Toward evening, my friend announced: "Come, let's go and see the bullfight." But I needed a cigar for that, and so I went into the first tobacco shop I saw, where the shopkeeper barked out: "A cigar, sure, but which one? What kind do you want?"—"Whichever you like, as long as it lasts through six bulls." In the arena, people were crammed into the stone tiers; the ring spread out at our feet, a pale disk surrounded with red by a bright barrier of painted boards. Nothing could trouble its calm orderliness: not the shouts and gesticulations of the crowd, not the music started up by the brass band, not the succession—by turns measured and frenzied—of figures formed and dissolved by the men in glittering costumes around the bull, a black, brutal monster overflowing with vigor, and yet so quickly killed. When the mules dragged away its body, the blood inscribed a long red comma on the sand; men quickly raced forward with rakes to erase it, so that nothing would come to disturb the placid surface that reflected the glory and triumph of the killer of bulls. Everything delighted me, the movements that won roaring ovations as well as those that elicited boos, and I paid as much attention to the long ash on my cigar as to the horn of the animal, appearing and disappearing in the undulating folds of the pink and yellow capes. Already the fifth bull was charging out of the depths of the arena. The man who had to kill it was, apparently, famous for his talent, the purity of his style and of his movements. When the bull stopped, panting, nervous, confused, he provoked it from very far away, almost the opposite side of the red circle, before moving forward with tiny steps, stiff and with his back arched, using his voice and his cape to encourage the animal to charge, which it always ended up doing; then, motionless, feet together and chest proudly flung out, the man would calmly make the animal flow around him, like a current eddying around a rock. I had, of course, had the rules of the game explained to me: nothing required the man to remain in place, to offer his belly or his loins to the horn, so close sometimes that it snagged the gilt decorations on his costume; it was a question of etiquette, which in this affair was everything; wounds or death weren't taken into consideration. And now the man was getting ready to kill the bull; drawn up onto the tips of his toes, turned sideways, he was aiming his long curved sword at the back of the bull's neck, straight between the horns of the exhausted animal, doomed but still raging; his left hand with its piece of red flannel crossed in front of his body, he dove straight in; a moment later, he was bouncing on the horns, a limp puppet, a rag doll, grotesque in his beautiful gilt costume, as if he were to remain caught up there forever, while his assistants rushed in shouting and vainly waving their capes. Finally he fell to the ground, the men drove the animal back, others tried to carry away the wounded man; "It's nothing," he seemed to say as he got up and grasped the sword held out to him, "it's nothing." He returned to stand facing the bull. His face, his hands, his shining outfit were coated in blood; arched back, in profile, he held his sword up with his fingertips, in a perfect triangle with his arm, as if to salute his adversary, and he stared at it with two round, black eyes, empty of all thought except the perfection of the gesture to be repeated, eyes that gazed at the animal to be killed the same way they would have gazed at a mirror. Then he made one swift gesture, and already he was turning his back on the staggering bull, dragged into the ballet of capes thrown under its muzzle, the sword planted to the hilt in its neck; he walked away without turning back, toward the red barrier, as the animal collapsed heavily behind him, its four hooves in the air, pointed at the sky.

That night, I found myself in a cellar; on a stage in the back, some men dressed in black, sitting on simple wooden chairs, their feet flat on the stage, were playing music. It was very beautiful; but to tell the truth, what I especially liked was the curtain drawn behind them, a long curtain with folds of garnet velvet, illumined with a bright light. Someone had handed me a drink, red also, in a tall, straight glass, I didn't really know what it was, wine perhaps; I was sitting at a little round table, in the company of many people, I didn't quite know who they were; my friend must have been there, but maybe he had gone away. After a while, a few young women came out onto the stage, wearing long black dresses spangled with red dots, like fat blood-red moons scattered across a night sky; they danced with stiff movements, yet their stiffness was strangely supple, forming and then unmaking squares and circles; when they twirled, upright and proud, their ample skirts flew around their fine muscular legs, opening up into large fluid circlets, like the wheel of a cape spun out behind his back by a haughty matador ending a series of passes by bringing his bull to its knees. The women stood out from the red curtain like shadows, they whirled round clicking their heels; they were made even more present by these rhythmic sounds and the figures they formed, static, almost clumsily linked figures, like the poorly connected passes of a novice still unsure of his animal, than by their bodies eclipsed behind the cloth of the moon-dresses; only the sweat soaking their armpits, visible when they raised their arms to snake their wrists around and snap their fingers, reminded one from time to time of their materiality. I was slowly getting drunk, and this drunkenness made me euphoric; yet at the same time, just like the bullfighter's gestures in the center of the arena's red circle, just like the movements of the dancers on the rectangle of the stage, it too, I realized, was a form of communion, the step beyond that imperceptibly opens up the road to the world of death, revealing to the one taking it that it already stretches far behind him, and always has.

I returned to the arena; beneath the flaming wheel of the sun, the red barrier was gleaming, its sweeping curve diagonally sliced by the line of shadow. Yet I passed from one circle to the other: for when I plunged my gaze into the circle formed by the arena, I finally found myself faced not with the bull and its horns, but with myself, my pale, distraught face, reflected in the dull halo of the mirror in my bedroom; and the flesh the bull's horn gouged, when it caught the unfortunate matador in the muscular triangle inside the thigh, almost by chance and in exactly the same way I sometimes happened to catch the soft, vulnerable triangle of a girl chance drove into my arms, this flesh then was in a way probably none other than my own, offered naked, without any protection—neither the ridiculous covering afforded by lace underwear, nor the dazzling and sovereign protection signified by the matador's fabulous suit of light—possibly only the protection of endless desire, flitting back and forth like a muleta shaken by the wind, a bloody, elusive, derisory rag, confusing all these forms into one impossible gesture, only to separate them forever.

In my bedroom, I would spend hour after hour resting, lying on my mattress, the curtains drawn but the French door wide open, letting the breeze play over my bare skin. My head turned to the wall, the round mirror reminded me of its presence; it no longer reflected my body, but its circle was filled with the dark, rumpled folds of the curtain, constantly agitated by the wind. When some need or other came over me, I would get up. The water, stretched out far beyond my windows, drew me; all of a sudden, I desired it passionately, frantically, but this desire brought with it neither the patience to leave the city again, nor the courage to confront the crowds and the noise and dirtiness of the beaches at the bottom of the streets. Further along, though, up the little hill, there was a swimming pool, a simple solution to these difficulties, and to get there, the metro. At one stop, a young couple came and sat down next to me, first the boy, then, on his lap, her back to his chest, the girl. She wore white overalls cut short and was greedily devouring a banana; from the side, I could see her freckles, she seemed rather ordinary, but lively and high-spirited. I couldn't see the boy at all: with his hand, he was caressing his friend's belly, and at each movement his smooth, downy arm brushed against my own, as if we were all three taking part in this affectionate gesture, as if without consulting each other they wanted to include me with them, and I was delighted at this, I was grateful to them for this friendly presence. The girl had finished her banana; taking advantage of another stop, she leaped out of the car to throw away the skin, then quickly flung herself back inside, laughing, and returned to slide down onto the legs of the boy, who resumed his caresses. Their image was reflected in the rectangle of the window opposite, I observed the girl, now slumped back in her man's arms, leaning on him with all her weight, happy. At the pool, a large open-air blue square overlooking the city, I gaily plunged my body into the cool, clear water; as I paddled about, or leaned on the edge, my eyes could run over the vast expanses of buildings, piles of blocks confusedly heaped up by a clumsy child, or else, drifting on my back, I could lose myself in the immense wavering dome of the sky. All around me rang out laughter, happy shouts, the sounds of water; bare bodies glistened in the sun; nearby, in another pool, bold, graceful children were attempting acrobatic dives from high diving boards of various heights. They always dove in groups, the girls with the girls and the boys with the boys; their temerity filled me with wonder: never would I have been capable of such beautiful, precise, courageous movements. When I climbed out of the water, I sat down still dripping at a little round table and ordered a dish of lime sorbet; I let the sun dry me as I ate the ice and watched the children dive. Two little girls had placed themselves at the edge of the highest diving board, a dozen meters above the water, with their backs to the pool, their arms alongside their body, their little muscles distinct and taut: as if on cue, they simultaneously let themselves topple backward into the void, stiff as boards; suspended in mid-air, they slowly unfolded their arms to form a point above their heads, just in time to break the surface of the water like a powerful arrow. Already other laughing kids were taking their place, I happily finished my sorbet, with each little spoonful savoring the wait before returning to the sweetness of the water.

My friend had invited me to celebrate his birthday. Reaching the foot of his building, I rang several times at the number I had been told: finally, an oldish-sounding lady replied, in a reedy, almost inaudible voice: "It's not here."—"But this is the address I was given!" I said indignantly.—"I know, you're not the first one. But it's not here."—"Where is it, then?"— "I don't know." In fact, it was the apartment right across the landing; shrewdly, I waited in the street, smoking, until other people arrived to show me the way. "Ah, you brought something to drink, excellent!" my friend exclaimed, brushing off my complaints about his mistake: "It's nothing, it's nothing." The apartment was small, the crowd dense, noisy; people were drinking, talking, there was no music. I didn't know many people here, no one actually, aside from my friend. But the people were drunk and excited and it wasn't difficult to strike up a conversation with them. I found myself talking with a young woman, a Russian. She was drinking a lot and laughing, a brittle laugh, but an agreeable one; one of her white arms had a series of scars on it, thick uneven strokes, which she told me she had inflicted herself, without really explaining either how or why in a way I could make sense of. But maybe she didn't really want to say. A fat blond woman, rather vulgar, had come in and was kissing her; this was her mother, already drunk, accompanied by a much younger man, his goatee carefully trimmed. "My stepfather," the Russian girl smirked; I went on drinking. In the hallway, another woman, the mistress of the house I think, caught me by the neck and greedily kissed my mouth. I gently pushed her away. "No? You don't want to?" She gave me a startled, frightened look.—"No," I replied, smiling kindly, "I don't want to."—"It's nothing," she snapped, continuing heavily toward the kitchen. In the living room, the Russian girl's mother was emitting loud, guttural laughter and shaking her full breasts in front of her companion's dazzled gaze. Her daughter was sitting at a low table; together with two of her friends (twins, seemingly identical, but who revealed surprisingly contrary characters as soon as you talked to them—one gentle, attentive, and patient, the other harsh, almost enraged, nursing a secret resentment that cast a shadow over all her words), she was taking cocaine, indifferent to her mother who was toying with her lover's curly hair and drinking. She was drinking too, methodically, she must have already been completely drunk yet she remained lucid, clear, friendly. I too was probably very drunk, like her. She spoke to me a lot; yet she didn't seem especially interested in me, she would disappear suddenly in the middle of a sentence, leaving me with her two friends or else my friend. I tried to talk with him, but he was completely incoherent, I couldn't understand anything. His brother, who was seven years younger than he but whose birthday we were also celebrating—one was born before midnight, the other after, and we had thus moved seamlessly from one birthday to the other—was nodding and chuckling knowingly; from time to time, he would take a little packet out of his pocket and pour some cocaine onto the table, inviting the guests to help themselves with a sweeping gesture. When I could, I resumed my conversation with the Russian girl. Her mother had disappeared, the woman who had wanted to kiss me was slumped next to the table, staring at me with mean and greedy eyes, I responded with a smile and kept talking with the girl. She was looking for more to drink. All the bottles were empty, now she was grabbing the glasses left on the table and without hesitating poured their contents into her own, laughingly mixing the different wines and drinking without respite. Finally, I managed to convince her to leave. In the street, the sky was turning pale, she immediately dragged me into a bar where I bought her several drinks; she had moved on to beer, while I was still drinking shots of vodka. When she looked at me, curiously, her pupils reflected not just my face, puffy and sagging from drink, but also seemed framed by the reflection of the window behind me, two little black marbles set in two luminous squares. I was trying to convince her to come back to my place, but she gently yet firmly refused my offers; she was filled with alcohol and cocaine, they made her thin body vibrate with a wicked joy; yet she remained completely in control of herself: "That's not how it's done," she said with a clear, slightly broken laugh. I laughed along with her, we understood each other very well. Outside, it was daylight. As I got into the taxi, I offered at least to drop her off on the way, but she refused this too and finally pushed me somewhat abruptly into the car. As it was starting up she walked off with long strides, waving a last goodbye with a broad, brittle smile, fragile and happy.

I rapidly developed a vivid passion for this girl. I would call her on the phone, and we would chat about trivial, inconsequential things; she always kept the same friendly distance. I invited her to the pool: she refused, citing an allergy to chlorine, and nothing could convince her to go to the sea. At night, we would get drunk together. She was learning Persian: happy at this incongruous pretext, I held forth on the evolution of the Indo-European languages, a subject I actually knew not much about, but enjoyed a lot. Sometimes, in her confident, precise way, she would interrupt me and abruptly go on to a different, completely unrelated subject; an hour later, just as abruptly, she would come back to it, only quickly to drop it again. While she spoke, I would look at her. She was not, strictly speaking, pretty; but the ease and confidence with which she inhabited her body and face delighted me. Her laughter pealed, the glasses and the ice clinked, the lighters scraped and clacked, the coins jingled on the zinc of the round tables, oh, sweet idyll. At the end of the night, she would always leave me in the same way, cordial, laughing, firm and cheerful.

To tell the truth, it wasn't really this girl I loved, but another one. I had dreamed of her one night, alone in the my high room, a long, tender, profound dream that swelled me with so much happiness that my awakening was like a sword-blow to the neck, inflicted with precision by the pitiless day. She was dark-haired, this I am pretty sure of, dark-haired and full of friendship and joy and madness; I didn't know who she was, I had never seen her before, nonetheless I knew her, I was certain of this, and she too knew me and was waiting for me, in the meantime whiling away her days however she could, freely making use of her body and her time and her beauty, which should have been saved for me, her sad knight of Aquitaine. She did nothing to please or displease me, and it was all the same to me; her friends and her lovers, big joyous violent men, I ignored them and never invited them into my home. I had known others like them, before, in the East, during bloody wars that resembled festivals, I had laughed and drunk with them while they killed each other, keeping my opinions to myself, always free. That may be why she had loved me: but I had never received anything from her, either good or bad, she had never granted me any rights or done me any wrongs; what she had given me, she had given freely, just as she had taken it back from me, and there was nothing to say to that, even though I was burning from head to foot, in a fire of ice that left no ash. At the same time I couldn't have cared less about her. I had met another girl, far nicer and more beautiful, a girl both lively and amusing, her superior by far. This was on the occasion of yet another celebration, a great popular festival, the streets were swarming with people, their bodies sweaty, happy and tired, who scattered like sparrows before the onslaught of columns of roaring devils, armed with wheels of fire that sprayed fans of sparks all around, followed by drummers lined up in rows as they steadily beat out the measure, frenzied, throbbing, maddening; behind them, the crowd formed again, laughing, jostling each other, whirling round, and then it all began all over again. I spent the night dancing with this girl I didn't know; one by one, the people around us left, overcome by exhaustion and alcohol. In the morning, I brought her back to my place, but instead of putting her in my bed, I took her in my arms and toppled with her onto the sofa, overwhelmed by uncontrollable laughter. I kissed her and she kissed me too, laughing too and protesting softly, I caressed and breathed in her long wavy hair, her beautiful lively body, I kissed her neck, the back of her neck, her little ear. When my hand tried to slip into her pants, though, she seized my wrist, with a firm and calm gesture; I kept insisting, between kisses I slipped my fingers here and there, then slowly returned to the elastic; once again, she put up a gentle but unshakable resistance. Finally I began caressing her through the thin fabric of her pants, beneath which I could feel the rougher texture of her underwear; she let herself go, her breathing caught in her throat, giving way to a long happy moan. I was happy too, for making her happy filled me with delight, I kept rubbing her delicately, she moved slowly beneath me, following in little circles the patient rhythm of my fingers, and I closed my eyes and plunged my face into her beautiful fragrant hair, right next to her ear, drinking in its smell mingled with the faint, acrid smell of her sweat, as very slowly her hands came down and undid my belt and pants, unhurriedly, button by button, and freed my cock to hold it between her palms, caressing it lightly, with minute movements, just for the pleasure of feeling it between her fingers as pleasure gripped her young body.

To this story, there's nothing else to add. Not really knowing where it comes from, I don't know what it means, or to whom it could be addressed; already, it is showing me to the door; nothing remains now but for me to send it to someone, who will send it to someone else, further on somewhere, with no hope of a return, no hope of a counter-key that could put an end to my dispossession. At the very most I would have liked it to leave behind the taste of lime sorbet, cool, light, tart, enjoyed in sunlight at the edge of a large pool, in the clear water of which bathers plunge their bodies just as you plunge into the bitterness of life, without looking back.

In Quarters

The outbursts of the children's laughter were so shrill that I gave up reading. Sighing, I closed the book on my finger and, discouraged, leaned my head back on the chaise longue. The laughter kept erupting, followed by a long, piercing scream; from inside the house came calls, women's voices. I closed my eyes and tried to concentrate on the tingling sensation in my face, warmed by the sun. But it was useless and I opened my eyes again. I was sitting at the back of the garden; at my feet, the grass glowed gently, a large triangle of light against the darker green of the hedge and the tall, dense trees outlined against the white sky, their leaves moving in a light breeze. Behind me, a chaotic stampede was approaching, interrupted by shouts of joy; a child rushed past my chaise, overturning the little table on which I had rested my glass, fortunately empty. I sighed again, set my feet on the ground and bent over to straighten the table and replace the glass. I also put down my book, whose mint-green cloth binding stood out like a small, luminous rectangle on the dark wood of the table. Nearby, the children were rolling on the grass, shout-ing; a little further away, a little blond girl wearing a short mustard yellow dress was watching them pensively, lying on her stomach and resting on her elbows, a long blade of grass in her teeth. I skirted round them all and entered the house. In contrast to the daylight the rooms seemed plunged in darkness; momentarily blinded, I blinked my eyes as I groped my way along the long hallway. The sun fell slanting through the tall windows and traced fine blades of light on the waxed floor. Undecided, I walked my fingers over the cream-colored wallpaper, its floral motifs interlaced with gilt threads, before pausing in front of a framed reproduction representing a haughty young lady from the past, her face pale and severe like an ivory mask pinned over all emotion, hiding forever the secret movements of her body. Once again, the children's laughter resounded toward the back of the hallway, came closer; everything seemed solid to me, much too solid. I entered a room, chose a book at random and sat down on the edge of the bed. Above the ornate brass headboard there hung a painting, an original work this time, showing a group of people dressed in dark brown, pink and white, scattered throughout a shady garden. A girl, seated, looked sideways at the spectator; another, laughing, was leaning her head and her crossed hands on the powerful shoulder of a man in a jacket; the cloth of her thin summer dress, artfully painted, hinted at a supple, agile body, which held itself in a curious torsion, one leg under the other, as if she were about to spin round with a leap to make her dress swirl around her hips. I opened the book and leafed through it, distracted by the cries resounding behind the door, piercing shouts of glee interlaced with childlike laughter, mingled from time to time with snatches of adult voices, amused or scolding, first quite close and then further away, lost in the depths of the vast house. A child came in, a blond boy with short hair, also looking for a book. He didn't so much as look at me; I watched him in silence as he searched through the library, roughly pushing back the volumes he didn't want until he finally made his choice, and then left without a word. Was he my child? In all honesty, I couldn't have said. I looked at the pages of my book, but the words floated in front of my eyes, empty of meaning. Finally I put it down on the embroidered bedspread and went out too, continuing down the hallway to the big living room. A little girl, maybe the same one from before, maybe another, was speeding toward me, her bare feet hammering on the floor; she crashed into my leg, burst out laughing, and continued on her way without pausing. In the living room, the blond boy was reading at a table, between two large windows through which light flooded in; his golden hair shone, but his serious, focused face was in shadow, and I couldn't see his eyes, fixed on the open pages. In front of him on the table was a large bowl of fruit; without lifting his head, he reached out, grabbed a plum, brought it to his lips, and bit into it, sucking in the juices. A little above his head, between the windows, hung a canvas in a simple wooden frame, a pensive girl in a pink blouse, seated at a long table, holding a peach. The interior, very white with dark, understated furniture, resembled the one in which I found myself; but this girl with her gaze at once serene and playful had her place there, whereas I was wandering like a shade among these quarters full of life. Near me, sitting with a cat on a long burgundy leather sofa, two young women were chatting as they drank their tea: "Did you see the weather report?"—"Yes, they were predicting rain."—"It doesn't look like it, though." The cat, purring, stretched and then fell asleep quite suddenly, its pointy head resting on its two outstretched paws. I walked a little forward, to the center of the big red rug that filled the room; they continued talking without paying attention to my presence, I hesitated, tracing with my foot the black and white patterns, interlaced with blue, on the rug, then moved almost backwards toward the large buffet that stood in the rear of the living room and poured myself a cup of tea. It was still hot; I set down the heavy ceramic teapot and blew on the cup as I listened absent-mindedly to the two women's chatter; my gaze wandered among the different paintings that decorated the room, going from one to the other and then back again, until it finally came to rest again on the child with the sun-filled hair. Absorbed in his reading, he wasn't paying any attention to what was around him, neither to me nor to the two women conversing and laughing, one of whom might have been his mother. His gaze, running over the printed lines of the book, perceived nothing but a flood of internal images, much more real and absorbing for him than anything in this house; at the same time, though, he was living his child's life in perfect harmony with this setting, the large, airy, luminous rooms of the vast house were like an extension of his small body, as varied and mysterious as his moods. As for me, I watched these people around me, I watched them attentively, but they remained out of my reach, like an image seen through a glass pane; even if I pressed my face against it, it was impossible to pass beyond it, to break this invisible surface or, on the contrary, to plunge into it as into an expanse of cold water; and behind it, things, equal to themselves, arranged themselves in a great mute tranquility, a harmonious design of colors, light, and movements, which organized into one single peaceful but inaccessible image blond child, sleeping cat, chatting women, and the young girl with the peach.

At dinner, it was more of the same. The children shrieked, guffawed, giggled, spilled their glasses on the table, wiped their mouths with their sleeves or rubbed oily fingers on their pants, the women scolded them, wiped them off, then served them more, all in a continuous racket of cutlery, dishes, and noisy chewing. If I wanted some wine, I had to wait for someone to serve another person to try to catch a few drops in passing, my glass stretched across the table; to eat, I pricked the tip of my fork haphazardly into neighboring plates, a green bean here, a piece of meat there, no one seemed to notice. From time to time, taking advantage of a brief pause in the conversation, I timidly hazarded a sentence, but it went unnoticed, the flow of words and shouts continued ceaselessly. The children got up with a loud scraping of chairs, went off to play, then came back to eat standing up before they were made to sit down; they drank while letting juice dribble down onto their chins and shirts, dug their hands into their plate to throw unwanted pieces into their neighbor's plate, then leapt up again to return to their games, deaf to any orders. For dessert, everyone rushed to the living room with his piece of cake; overwhelmed, I quickly swallowed some leftovers abandoned on the plates as the table was cleared around me. In the living room, visitors were arriving; they were served drinks and cigarillos as they struck up conversation interlaced with pleasantries and flatteries; I looked for a chair, so I could at least sit down and listen, but in vain, none was free; it seemed better to withdraw. I found myself in a large, completely white and blue bathroom; three little girls were splashing about and laughing in a great bathtub filled with bubbles, but as I tried to pass by, they began squealing and waving their arms, sending huge sprays of water through the room that forced me to step back to keep from getting soaked. The blond child was playing the piano in another room, a simple little nursery rhyme whose notes he picked out as he marked time under his breath. I wanted to reach out and play a few notes with him; without noticing me, he slammed the lid down on my fingers and rushed out in a noisy clatter of footsteps. I opened the piano and tried to sketch out the beginning of a piece, but my swollen hands no longer remembered the fingerings. Above the piano, the portrait of an old, noble-looking and somewhat bitter man contemplated me with an air of reproach, his lips pinched as if to let me know I had no place here. Fatigue overwhelmed me, I decided to go to bed; but I didn't know where to sleep: I visited several bedrooms, all equally clean and handsome, and finally chose one at random. I got undressed at the foot of the bed, carefully folding my clothes, which I arranged on a chair; as I slipped under the sheets, I glimpsed the reflection of my body in the large round mirror hanging opposite the bed, a white body, seemingly in good shape, but as if completely foreign to me. I put out the light and stretched out on my side, one hand under my cheek, the other pressed against my chest. But I couldn't manage to find sleep. Through the wooden door more children's shouts resounded, the noise of footsteps, bursts of voices. They seemed to come from all sides of the house, moved from one place to the other, grew distant, then returned all at once to swoop down on me. Merriment had turned into anger, I heard weeping, curt, gruff phrases, but didn't know what they were about. Things calmed down, then started up again; finally the voices grew brighter, more cheerful. A woman laughed in fits and starts, a man joined in, the children too laughed calmly in another part of the house. A little later on—I still wasn't sleeping— the door opened and a bright light streamed from the chandelier on the ceiling. I squeezed my eyes shut and burrowed into the pillow. Nearby, someone was getting undressed; I heard the rustle of cloth, then the sound of a brush being pulled through long hair. Finally the person slid into the bed next to me and, turning its back to me, switched the light off. From her smell, I understood it was a woman; her body, warm and soft, surrendered itself quickly to sleep, her breathing became even, then filled with a very slight snore. Annoyed, I turned onto my back and opened my eyes. Little by little, they grew used to the darkness; shifting them to the side, I could just make out the curve of the sheet, drawn over the woman's shoulder, and the dark mass of her hair. Once again, I looked at the ceiling, examining in the penumbra the long oak beams and the chandelier, whose cut glass facets on yellow brass branches caught vague luminous reflections. The woman next to me slept without moving; the sheets rose and fell to the regular rhythm of her breathing. But sleep continued to elude me, my anxious thoughts refused to grant it to me. When finally I saw the sky grow pale behind the window, I rose soundlessly and dressed in the half-light.

The woman had turned onto her back; I could make out her arm under the sheet stretched out across her belly, her hand nestled between her legs. I went out and gently closed the door. I soon got lost in the disorder of the rooms: in one, four children were sleeping in bunk beds, their little heads barely protruding from the sheets and the piles of stuffed animals; in another, an old woman was snoring, tucked in a narrow iron bed pushed against the wall; even further on, there was a couple, the head of the woman nestled in the hollow of the man's shoulder, the embroidered sheet thrown back, revealing a white breast with a large pink areola, milky against the darker chest on which it rested. In the hallways, already lit by daylight, dusty paintings stood out from the darkness, outlining little rectangles of color on the walls covered with eggshell, pale green and off-white cloth, enhanced by brown or gold. Finally I found the way out and slipped through the door, which I closed carefully on the sleeping house, taking care not to disturb anyone.

The gate locked behind me with a gentle click and I emerged into the pale dawn. The road was wet from the streetcleaners' trucks; along the sidewalk, the still-hesitant leaves of the plane trees masked a whitening sky streaked with yellow and orange glints. I walked with a carefree step, examining with a burst of pleasure the cement of the sidewalk, applied in grand, sweeping strokes, as if with a paintbrush, then broadening my gaze to take in the greys of the pavement, the façades of the houses and the vanilla-marbled trunks of the plane trees, the absinthe-green of the leaves in the glow of early morning, the coral red, navy blue, canary yellow, or white of the parked cars. When I reached the building, I inserted my flat key into the lock high up in the heavy wooden door, and leaned on it with all my strength to push it open and penetrate the narrow entrance hall. Already I felt more vigorous: I was regaining solidity, my body was finding its forms and limits and was once again occupying space. In front of me stood the door, painted olive green, of an always absent neighbor; to my right, the lavender-colored stairway, covered in a worn old red plush carpet fixed to the steps by small brass bars, led to the landing where my doors were. There, I hesitated between the one on the left, painted black, and the one on the right, a cardinal red; but my reinvigorated body was reminding me of its own demands, and I made an about-face and went back out into the street, in search of an open café. A little further up there was a small square lined with plane trees; a waiter in a black vest with gold stripes was setting out onto the sidewalk some round greenish marble tables and little straw-colored wicker chairs, woven with red and black, two of which were already occupied by men in dark coats. One of them was reading the paper, whose headline, of which I could see only half, mentioned a country known for its hostility to us; the other suddenly raised his head: under the brim of his soft hat, tinted, tortoise-shell glasses masked his gaze. I entered the café as the waiter was placing two small white cups in front of them, and ordered a coffee and some buttered toast, which I ate slowly at the counter before having another coffee and smoking a cigarette, happily enjoying the rediscovered feeling of my body.

Outside, at the street corner, I glimpsed a shadow behind one of the plane trees. I leaped over and seized it by the wrist: "What do you want? What are you doing here? Are you spying on me?" She glared rebelliously at me and tried to free her arm, but I held it firmly. "Come with me." Without letting her go, I brought her back to the apartment; she followed me unprotesting to the sky-blue door, which stood out from afar in the midst of the building's wide, dirty brick façade. Opening it, I noticed that the paint was peeling: It needs repainting, I said to myself as I pushed in the door, perhaps in a color that matches the stairway better. I pulled the girl, who was still not protesting, up the steps to the narrow landing, where once again I hesitated in front of the two doors. Finally I chose the one on the left, the black one. The room was dark until I turned on the light: everything, the furniture, the floor, the loft where the bed was, was covered in large plastic sheets, dirty but transparent. One of the sheets, draped over a stool, formed a bulge on which a set of building blocks was placed, an assemblage of red, yellow, blue, black, and white pieces, the only touch of color in this grey, abandoned room, a room that looked as if it were waiting for repairs forever delayed. I contemplated the window with dismay; behind it the white wall of the air shaft gleamed weakly. "So, the other room, then," I finally conceded with regret, without looking at the girl who remained silent. This room was more open, I could see right away; the window, here, looked out on a brick wall, so close you could almost touch it, but the long narrow room didn't look dark, and it suited me. The walls were pale, they must once have been white, but time had stained and dirtied them, you could even see indistinct traces of color, and they were covered in pictures, photographs, newspaper clippings, old sepia prints, pages torn from books, tacked on or stuck there with yellowed Scotch tape. I had no idea who could have assembled this clutter of images, perhaps another tenant, perhaps me, at another time, hard to say. Near the door stood a blondwood board resting on metal trestles, on which lay scattered a few books, most of them with their covers torn off, and some piles of papers; on the other side, a low, round table with a chair occupied the space in front of the bed, so wide that it left only a narrow passageway to reach the bathroom door, painted the same red as the entry door. I motioned the girl to the bed: "Go on, lie down there." She skirted round me with a childlike laugh and crossed the mahogany-colored floor as if she had no feet; in front of the bed, she spun round in a fluid motion and let herself fall back, her arms outstretched, scattering her Venetian blonde hair on the lilac expanse of the sheets, without taking off her apple-green raincoat, which revealed smooth, slim legs. I sat down at the round table, poured myself a drink from a bottle there, and lit a cigarette. The girl laughed in crystal-clear tones and leapt up. "You're funny!" she laughed. She let her raincoat slip to the bed; underneath, she wore a short, eggplant-colored summer dress, chiffon possibly, which barely reached below her upper thighs. She ran her fingers through her thick shoulder-length hair and walked lightly forward. I stretched out my hand to caress her thigh in passing, but she smoothly dodged it, and my fingers just grazed the thin, rustling cloth of her dress as she slipped behind the desk and began playing with the papers, leafing carelessly through the piles. "Don't touch," I scolded, amused.—"Why don't you offer me a drink?" she asked, smiling, still looking at the papers. I poured her a glass and brought it to her; she drank a mouthful and suddenly raised her large, dark eyes to me, deep and laughing. "Will you run me a bath?"—"Run it yourself," I retorted rudely, sitting back down at the round table. She burst out laughing, straightened up and crossed the room, undoing the hooks on the back of her dress, which she slipped smoothly over her head and threw onto the sheets to join the green raincoat. Aside from the dress, she wore nothing but a pair of tiny, salmon-colored panties made of an almost transparent tulle; I admired the long curve of her back, the radiance of her golden skin, the slender nape of neck under her short hair. "You are a boor!" she called out to me before turning round, hands on her hips. "Do you think I'm beautiful?" she went on, her laughter intensifying. Her brown nipples stood out on small breasts, I could make out her thick pubic hair under the thin cloth of the panties; she fluffed out her hair with her hands and smiled wide, young, splendid, and proud. I didn't say anything, happy simply to look at her. "Boor!" she repeated, still laughing. She opened the bathroom door and busied herself near the enamel bathtub; water gushed out from the big white faucets. I watched her through the half-open door: she straightened up, took off her panties, lifting first one foot, then the other; then she disappeared from my sight and I heard a liquid tinkling, softer and shriller than the jet gushing out of the faucets. As the sound continued I let my gaze wander over the photographs covering the walls. There were some strange images: a pregnant woman walking proudly in front of soldiers standing at attention; a crowd of men massed together, fists raised, each with a striped cover tied across his shoulder; two men in black suits standing in front of a hedge, multicolored umbrellas raised above their heads, the lower part of their faces covered with surgeons' masks. One of the images in particular held my attention: an Asiatic soldier, in the midst of a crowd wearing old-fashioned oriental outfits, was completing a sweeping movement with his sword as the head of a condemned man kneeling in front of him lifted from his shoulders, in a thick spurt of blood. It was the perfect capture of a twofold instant, carried out like a sport: the one where the blade slices through the neck with a perfected gesture, synchro-nized with the one when the finger of the photographer presses the shutter release, the moment of the execution articulated with the moment of the creation of the image, the dreamed-of, unprecedented, fully achieved image, in all its banal repetition (for there were hundreds of such images, as I knew well), of the instant of a man's death. Still perched on the shoulders, the head hesitated, the mouth deformed in a silent cry and the eyes closed to the unfathomable fact, just as the condemned man's life hesitated, still and forever suspended in the brief click of the shutter. The girl, naked, had emerged from the bathroom, and was idling in front of the bed vigorously brushing her teeth, like a little girl, a thin film of white foam on her lips. She glanced over at me, smiled through the foam, then returned to the bathroom. I finished my cigarette while gazing once again at the image of the decapitated Chinese man, then went to join her. She was already lying in the bathtub; the water, still agitated, blurred the lines of her body; only her narrow face and the tips of her breasts rose above the bluish water. "Yes, you are beautiful," I sadly acknowledged as I sat on the edge to test the temperature of the water.

When it came down to it, I liked this girl. She was cheerful, light-hearted, she said yes to everything. But something in her always escaped me. In my arms, naked, she trembled like a bird flapping its wings, my gestures drew from her body long sighs that became stifled moans, but no matter how much I touched her, caressed her, spread her supple limbs to burrow into her, I never managed to grasp her, and the feeling of her constantly slipped between my fingers. I came too, in long whitish streams on her golden skin, then I lay down next to her, gathered her in my arms, slept a little; when I woke up, everything began again, without end, without conclusion, without appeasement. When we spoke, she answered me laughing, with words as light as her, not really empty, but without any consistency, like a pleasant punctuation to my statements. We ate whatever fell into our hands, in bistros or diners chosen at random; I swallowed the dishes with appetite but without discernment, to regain my strength before I brought her back to the room. As for her, everything was the same to her, she took her pleasures without concern, in the lightness of the moment, at once greedy and indifferent. But she couldn't tell me anything, and I could never be sure of her, of her body or her words. Nonetheless, in this room with its walls covered with photographs, I felt entirely myself, a being equal to others, living its own life, according to the general rules, like everything that exists. Only the girl escaped this unexpressed harmony, her presence remained a constant dissonance, forever oblique.

Her very vivacity turned her into an apparition, a little moth that flutters between four walls and then dies in the dawn light. I never tired of her, it wasn't a question of that, but I didn't know what to do with her, where or how to place her to ensure even a temporary equilibrium, I ran into the angles of her small mobile body as into disjointed surfaces, unable to place her in the same space as me, even for an instant.

I joined my friends in the train compartment with some satisfaction. One of them had called me, laughing: "You haven't forgotten, have you? It's tomorrow morning, the train leaves at 8:43. I have your ticket."—"What's the weather like, there?"—"I don't know. They're still predicting rain, but for now it's nice." As I closed the red door of the room, I realized I hadn't brought a bag; as for the girl, I didn't really know where she was; it was possible that she had stayed in the bed, and that I hadn't seen her, or she might have left before me, I don't know. In front of the door to my building stood two men in dark suits: one, his foot resting on a step, was jotting something down in a notebook; the other stopped me for a second to ask for a light. On the way, I passed large modern apartment buildings, constructions of cubes with bluish, brown and rust tones, where the windows alternated with metal strips to form long vertical bands, divided in sections of varying width. The streets were getting crowded; I passed many people, men and women hurrying to work, lost in their thoughts; from time to time, however, a young woman would raise her eyes and smile at me, and I would return the favor, but it was rare. In the station's concourse a cheerful agitation reigned; my friends, in the compartment we had reserved, were trading books; I went to order a sandwich in the café car and settled on a tall stool. The train had gotten underway with a grinding noise, behind the window the city's buildings were already rushing by, then increasingly disorderly and dirty suburbs, which finally gave way to the first trees and to fields dotted with pretty little cemeteries. The sky was clear, luminous, streaked with long white contrails; in the distance a few clouds were gathering, casting large shapeless shadows on the fields of wheat and pale barley. It wasn't I who had chosen the destination but the friend who had called me the night before; she had enumerated the charms of this little provincial town one after the other, as well as the pleasure of the crowd that filled its streets at night, in this season: everything, she said, made it an ideal goal for our excursion. She had picked the hotel as well: my room was all white, with an ivory carpet and a white bedspread, a black leather chair, and as sole decoration the picture of a red square framed over the bed. The shower, tiled in white and grey, was roomy; I stood under the water with pleasure, vaguely regretting that the girl wasn't there, for this shower would have pleased her, I was sure of it; but I forgot this thought as soon as it had arisen, abandoning myself to the burning stream hammering the back of my neck.

My friends wished to visit a church, then go for a stroll; as for me, I opted for the museum, and agreed to meet up with them in the early evening. The sky, above the maze of narrow streets that led to the museum square, was turning grey, and I told myself I should have listened to the forecasts and brought an umbrella, or at least a raincoat. The museum, still little known, had just recently opened its doors: a local eccentric millionaire, whose only daughter, they said, had hanged herself, had left his collection to the city, along with a large enough endowment to ensure its preservation and exhibition. The rooms were not large, but they were tall and filled with light, white like my hotel room, which gave a feeling of space conducive to meditation. There weren't many visitors, the rare sounds remained hushed, even footsteps scarcely echoed on the waxed floor. I passed through these rooms aligned like chapels, casting my gaze over the images hanging there, most of which, in fact, said nothing to me. They were beautiful paintings, painted with talent and vigor; the figures, rendered according to all the rules of art, seemed endowed with life and movement, but they didn't speak to me, and I kept moving. I finally came to a halt in front of a large, almost square canvas, slightly taller than me, a red background on which was painted a large black rectangle, then below it another narrower rectangle, red too but darker than the background, and more irregular. This indeed was not much, but what struck me is that if you stood your ground for a moment as you contemplated them, these rectangles began to move, to float forward or to withdraw, vertiginously. When I stepped back a little, the black rectangle advanced gently toward me, as if it were inviting me to join it; but as soon as I took a step forward, it speedily withdrew and passed far behind the background, revealing itself as a gaping abyss into which I nearly fell. Overcome with fear, I would stumble back, and immediately it leaped forward, recovering in an instant its place suspended in front of the background, opening up to me with a light, silent smile. As for the lower rectangle, it evaded me more mischievously: for instance, if you took one or two steps to the side, it changed color, veering to orange, a more muted, slightly burnt color; otherwise, it danced from side to side, always a little behind the large black rectangle. This surprising painting acted as if it were the one looking at me, it was a face, smiling seriously and kindly, a face that was watching me watch it, without taking its gaze off me, preventing me from moving away or even looking elsewhere. Finally, a guard had to come over to tap me on the shoulder: "We're closing, sir, it's time." Freed by his intervention, I joined the last visitors heading for the exit. Outside, a few drops had begun to fleck the grey stone of the sidewalk; one hit me on the forehead, another on my hand. Just opposite, a store was closing its doors; the storekeeper, quite politely, allowed me to buy a felt hat from her before she pulled down her metal grate. On the square where I was supposed to meet my friends, the crowd was dense, compact and noisy, the first signs of rain discouraging neither its cheerfulness nor its animation. I found my friends at the covered terrace of a café and ordered a drink as they made fun of my hat, which, however, was quite practical. We drank and smoked as they described the church in detail; for my part I was silent, happy to hear the excited sound of their voices. When we left the bistro, the rain had intensified; umbrellas in the crowd unfurled one after the other and began to bump against each other, so that I sometimes had to duck my head to avoid being hit in the eye. Little by little, in the heart of this crowd, I lost sight of my friends; finally they disappeared altogether, and I found myself alone. I wasn't worried: It's not such a big town, I said to myself, I'll find them again soon. I was walking alongside a curved stone parapet; behind, I knew, flowed the river in whose bend the town nestled, but it was too dark on that side to see anything. Two men in raincoats were approaching me, walking at the same pace, their faces invisible beneath their large black umbrellas. I found their appearance vaguely threatening; but as they reached me, they separated without a word, passing on either side of me to join up again behind me. Further on, the street rose and widened, leading to a broad stone bridge that connected this bank to the new part of town; at the entrance to the bridge, I turned back, picking a narrow street that rose toward the squares further up. But I didn't find my friends there either. Dodgy-looking figures in long coats were clustered in little groups beneath the trees, whispering furtively; cars with tinted windows came and went in an incessant ballet; sometimes, one would pull up next to one of the groups, a door would open, a few words would be exchanged, or else a man would get in, slam the door, and the car would start up again. Above the streets and the little squares, lamps hanging from wires shone in the night, their gleam, under the now continuous rain, forming large, ovoid haloes. There are strange things going on here, I said to myself as I avoided these groups of suspicious-looking men; as for my friends, no matter how much I paced up and down the streets, there was no sign of them; as it got late, passersby grew more and more infrequent, but still I persisted, searching each corner with a growing feeling of unease. I thus found myself in a little park nestled between some old houses; tall old trees grew between the paths, perched on mounds surrounded by metal gates; set a little back, in a recess, one could make out the opening to a sort of bower, accessible by a few steps and feebly lit; I stuck my head in, in the vain hope of finding my friends chatting away, sheltered from the rain, but on the stone benches there were only three soldiers, in officer's uniforms with wet epaulets; they were smoking cigarettes and speaking loudly, without paying any attention to me. "Frankly, they're going too far," one of them was saying, his grey mustache, yellow with nicotine, quivering over his unpleasant mouth.—"Yes, that's for sure. They're provoking us," declared the second one, lifting his cap to scratch his forehead. "We can't let them get away with it," gravely concluded the third. "We have to react." I left them to their discussion and regained the street, profoundly discouraged. My hotel, I knew, wasn't far away; perhaps it would be better to go back and wait there, rather than wander like this in the rain. And also, all these sinister figures had me a bit worried. In fact, two of them, hands in pockets, were standing in front of the hotel; despite the night and the rain, which was still falling in small, thin droplets, they wore dark glasses, as if they were playing cops, or spies. I walked past the entrance without stopping; they followed me with their gaze, but didn't move. The street dipped down to join the main street; here the crowd grew thicker, but I kept catching glimpses of one of the sinister gentlemen standing beneath a tree or seated behind the window of a diner. At the end of the main street stood the station; a train was leaving within the hour, I bought a ticket and took a seat with relief, wiping with the back of my sleeve the damp felt of my new hat.

The rain streaked the train's windows; beyond, everything was dark, opaque, unreachable. It was still raining when I got out, a firm, sustained shower now; I reached my apartment soaking wet, a little annoyed. The girl, wearing nothing but cotton panties, chartreuse green with thin red stripes, was leafing through a magazine, lying on her belly on the lilac rectangle of the bed. "What are you doing here?" I asked, surprised, shedding my wet clothes. She smiled at me as I was struggling with my pants: "Well, I was waiting for you."—"You could have turned on the heat, at least," I grumbled. "It's freezing in here." Although she was nearly naked, she didn't seem to notice, whereas I was shivering; I hurried to pull on a dry pair of pants, then a shirt and a sweater. That didn't help much and I sat down at the round table to pour myself a drink. The girl had sat up and, sitting cross-legged, was looking at me with an amused air: her smile, her thin waist, her pert little breasts, the bones of her knees, everything in her was like a rebuke addressed to me, friendly and indistinct. Glass in hand, I rose and went to sit down behind the desk. The girl fell back, her head in the pillows, her knees touching and forming, with her feet flat on the violet sheets, an unstable triangle that she swung quietly from side to side. "Come here, if you're cold."—"No, not now," I answered distractedly as I fiddled with a pen and shifted some papers, running my gaze over the countless pictures adorning the walls without really seeing them. "Take a hot bath, then," she suggested. I rubbed my shoulders: "No, not now." A little glass egg, opaque and rather rough, had made its way into my fingers; I weighed it, slid it over my palm, then lifted it to the light: it glowed with a warm, red, dark, shifting light, as if it were filled with blood, or else incubating a mysterious creature intimately linked to fire. I finished my drink and looked around for the bottle, but the girl, I'm not sure how, had gotten hold of it and was rolling it between her legs, laughing: "You want it? Come and get it."—"Oh, you're annoying." My shoulders were shuddering in spasms: I must have really caught cold. The rain was still falling heavily behind the window, darkening the space, almost masking the brick wall even though it was quite close. I got up and headed for the bathroom; the girl had taken up her magazine again and was turning the pages, toying with the bottle between her feet. I stood in front of the mirror and examined my face: it looked strangely vague to me, half erased, I couldn't seem to grasp its workings; mystified, I rubbed it, but it was as if the skin were peeling away between my fingers, leaving me even more insubstantial. I preferred not to see this so I returned to the room; the girl was still reading, quite alive and absolutely real with her thin bones and delicate joints, her warm, golden skin, her hair with its reddish reflections, her dark, always slightly amused eyes. I was afraid of touching her, it seemed to me as if my fingers would pass through her skin, or else would crumble against her like wet sand. I returned to the desk after grabbing the bottle, poured myself another glass, and began reading the pages piled there. The handwriting was not at all unlike my own, I myself must have written these lines, these pages of text, but they said absolutely nothing to me, and I could barely grasp their meaning. It was a kind of story: the narrator, a lost shade, was wandering through a vast house whose rooms echoed with the laughter of small children. The setting seemed vaguely Russian, it could have been a story by Chekhov if it had had the slightest psychological substance; in any case, it had nothing to do with me. Perhaps it was a translation I had done and then forgotten? Or the copy of a text I had come across? I had no idea, and it didn't matter. On the bed, the girl seemed to be sleeping, her breasts hidden under the over-turned magazine, her head on its side, her face half masked by her hair. She is taking up more and more room, I said to myself, soon she'll be treating this place like her own. I was still very cold, my whole body was trembling, but I didn't want to lie down next to her, I was afraid of hurting myself on her sharp bones, her hard, piercing body; so I stacked the papers, went out into the hallway, and opened the second door, the one on the left. I crossed the room, walking on the plastic tarps, climbed the ladder to the loft, and slipped under the tarp that covered it, rolled into a ball, my eyes closed, my legs racked with long shivers. How long did this last? I couldn't say, an eternity of sand and lava, my body had rid itself of all solidity and all presence, it was floating very high up on the fever as if on a funeral barge, traveling over the years all the seas of the world, unable to find its way, neither toward life, nor toward death. When at the end of this centuries-long journey I opened my eyes, the tarp had disappeared; I was lying beneath a thick comforter wrapped in a beige cover, completely soaked with my sweat. I turned over and examined the room: all the tarps had been removed, the floor was covered in a thick sky-blue carpet spotted with dark blue patterns, everything looked crisp and clean, the colorful toy was still resting on the stool. Against the wall stood a tall rectangular mirror, set in a thin orange frame: I looked for my reflection in it, but could only see that of the toy, which looked bigger and more elaborate than the one I remembered, as if it had grown during the long night. I heard a door open under the loft, I had never noticed there was one, and the girl appeared on the blue carpet. This time, she wore a lightweight pair of dark-brown pants and a red tank top with a large black circle across the chest. "That's better, isn't it?" she said, raising her head toward me and smiling widely. "You should knock down the wall, or at least put in a double door, that would give you more space." I didn't have the strength to tell her to keep her advice to herself and I closed my eyes, rolling onto my back and stretching my aching legs. My clothes, I noticed only then, had disappeared along with the tarps, I was lying naked under the comforter, and I felt a sudden shame at this, as if I had been turned into a plucked bird, bristling and scared. "Where are my clothes?" I asked in a murmur, but if she heard me, she didn't reply, she had disappeared again. A vague sound of water reached me, she was probably running a bath, on the other side; all of a sudden, the sound became clearer, and even before she reappeared I understood that the mysterious door must communicate with the bathroom, allowing passage between the two contiguous rooms. This time, she was holding a green apple, which she brought to her nose before biting into it. She held out to me another one which she had kept hidden behind her back: "Here, take it." Since I didn't react, she insisted, shaking the apple almost in front of my face: "Go on, it'll do you good." I didn't move and she bit again into her own apple, chewing slowly and carefully as she slipped the other one into her pants pocket. "The bath will be ready. Are you coming?" I couldn't take my eyes away from the round ball on her hip; finally, I raised my eyes to the mirror, which reflected in its orange frame the long supple line of her body. "Where are my clothes?"—"Oh, what a pain you can be!" she laughed. "They're here, on a chair. I added some clean underwear, you hadn't put any on." She went back under the loft and closed the door. I listened to her busying herself behind the wall, she had turned off the water and must have been undressing, then I heard her body slide into the bath. She kept eating her apple; the water made little lapping sounds. Then I squirmed out from under the comforter and managed with difficulty to reach the ladder, which creaked beneath my weight as I somehow descended, holding on with all my strength so as not to fall. My clothes were indeed where she had said; but my hat was still in the other room, along with my jacket, wallet, and cigarettes. Yet passing through this bathroom, which I imagined completely overflowing with this girl's excess of life, was beyond me, and the key to the hallway door was precisely still in my jacket pocket. I tried to consider my situation, but my thoughts, foggy, kept shredding apart and contradicting one another in turn; the rain, still drumming in the air shaft, complicated things even more, since going out in the downpour in just a shirt was unthinkable, but as for confronting this impossible girl once again, I was incapable of it, and no other options presented themselves to me for the moment. I could have stayed there for a long time pointlessly turning over these thoughts, but every time I moved, the large mirror set against the wall sent back a reflection, too fragmented and aggressive to be my own, which put me ill at ease. Undecided, I opened the hallway door: a large tan canvas umbrella stood there, open and overturned, soaking the old red carpet with water. That solves everything! I exclaimed joyfully, grasping the black leather handle. Leaning against the railing, I shook it, sprinkling the carpet and the lavender floor with a rainfall of droplets, then closed it and started down the steps, leaning with all my weight on the handle in a vain attempt to control my legs which, lost, were each trying to move in a different direction.

Walking in the rain, my head and upper body well protected by the unfurled umbrella, I was overcome with a child-like happiness, albeit slightly tinged with anxiety: I looked around me, examining the trees and cars parked along the sidewalk, but I saw nothing out of the ordinary. The rare passersby, also protected from the downpour by umbrellas or sometimes just a newspaper held over their heads, walked quickly, each had his own goal and no one paid me any mind. Having reached the house, I unlocked the gate, and, closing it carefully behind me, crossed the small garden to ring the doorbell. My shoes and pant cuffs were soaked, but that didn't bother me; absentmindedly, ringing again, I noticed that I was already standing much more easily. A woman, no longer young, opened the door: "Oh, it's you! We were wondering where you were. The little one is sick." Closing the umbrella and placing it in the large stand meant for that purpose, I followed her down the hallway, decorated with reproductions, to the children's room, leaving traces of wet footsteps on the wooden floor. The boy was lying under several dark covers, curled up, his whole body shaking in long spasms. I reached out and touched his forehead, which burned beneath my fingers, then stroked his hair soaked with sweat. "Has the doctor come?" I asked, without turning, the woman who stood a little back at the entrance to the room.—"Yes. He gave him an injection."—"When?"—"It was this morning." I noticed a bottle of pills at the bedside, picked it up, read the label, and put it back down. "Did the doctor leave this?"—"Yes. He said to give him one every four hours."—"And that's been done?"—"Yes, you can count on us." Next to the medicine, on the low table, there was also a carafe of water and a glass; I carefully rolled the child onto his back and lifted his head, carrying the glass to his lips: "Drink," I said to him, "you have to drink." He didn't open his eyes but parted his lips; I brought the glass to them, but his mouth was trembling too much, the glass clinked against his teeth, the water dribbled down his chin. I put his head back onto the sweat-soaked pillow and stroked his hair again. "Bring me a basin of water. With a sponge, or a washcloth." The woman withdrew wordlessly, then returned with what I had asked for. I placed the basin on the floor, soaked the washcloth, squeezed it out, and, sitting on the edge of the bed, spread it over the child's forehead. He raised his hand and placed it over my own, it was as light as a cat's paw, dry and burning. I re-soaked the washcloth and repeated the gesture several times in a row; little by little, the long shivers began to calm down; finally, I managed to get him to drink a little. The woman, behind me, was watching me in silence. I got up and looked at her: "The sheets are soaking, his pajamas too. Change them. Can you do that?" She avoided my gaze and nodded. I went out and headed for the large living room. Several people were there, exchanging pleasantries without much conviction; at the table near the window, some children were listlessly playing cards, a few girls and another boy, younger than they; above their heads, the young lady in pink was still contemplating me with her calm, almost complicit gaze, as if she wanted to invite me to share her peach. I poured myself a glass of wine and took a seat on the sofa, crossing my legs and authoritatively grasping the hand of the woman seated next to me. Whenever a new subject was introduced, I gave my opinion in a firm, clear, decisive voice; the people gathered around me gravely nodded, without ever contradicting me. In the evening, the doctor came by; I had in the meantime washed and changed, and put on a clean suit with a vest and even a tie made of crocheted wool, brown like the suit. I accompanied the doctor to the boy's room and stood next to him as he examined him, auscultated him, and took his temperature. Several others had followed us into the room, women and men and even a little girl, they couldn't stand still but came and went aimlessly, without saying a word but fortunately keeping their distance. The doctor finally delivered his prognosis, which coincided exactly with my own: continue the pills and compresses, watch over the child, make him drink. "Did you hear that?" I called out to the people huddling around. "Make him drink, that's important, that's what I said." I thanked the doctor and escorted him to the front door; we separated with a frank handshake, and he promised to return the next morning, early.

During the meal, the banal, disjointed conversation continued; without arrogance but firmly, I discouraged useless discussions, put an end to pointless controversies with a fair opinion, warned off those who got too excited, supported those who spoke sensible words. It wasn't that I took myself so seriously, on the contrary, I felt like a kid playing at being an adult, but playing seriously, so seriously that no one suspected, and when I commented in detail on the grave foreign policy crisis brewing, everyone listened to me attentively, drinking in my words without interrupting me. The children ate in silence, with just a slight clink of silverware, at times asking politely, in the interludes between subjects, for salt, or water, or some more food. A boy brought his hand to his lips: I looked at him, he blushed and grabbed his napkin to wipe his face. Their meal over, the children excused themselves and cleared their places; I poured more wine for the grownups and handed out cigarillos to those who wanted them. The woman seated to my left, who kept her beautiful clear eyes fixed on me as she listened to my words in silence, raised a lighter and lit it; I brought her hand to the tip of my cigar, thanking her with a smile, holding her fingers delicately so the flame wouldn't tremble. She contemplated me with boundless gratitude, but at the same time a vague anxiety disturbed her gaze, making her indistinct and rarefying her features, just as was the case for all those gathered around this table. I heard a noise and raised my head: the blond child was standing in the doorway, his feet bare, pale as a sheet. I put my cigar down in the ashtray, got up, joined him and took him in my arms before heading for one of the empty rooms where I placed him on the embroidered bedspread. He murmured a few indistinct words, I brought my ear closer, the words took on strength and began to form phrases, I listened attentively, he spoke in a loud voice now, his eyes wide open and focused on a point that I couldn't locate, his words had become clear but I was incapable of grasping their meaning, he was uttering sentences whose syntax was impeccable but whose key word, the one that would give meaning to all the others, remained incomprehensible, a group of syllables seemingly significant but tied to nothing, or else there came a word perfectly comprehensible, obvious, but inserted into a completely scrambled sentence, incapable of supporting its signification. I spoke too, calm and peaceful words, I answered his statements without thinking, trying to bring him back to a sense of reality, but each time his words only placed themselves in the wake of mine in order to overtake them and then race away again in the opposite direction, to a dizzying distance, at the depths of which they turned round and came back, following the opposite path with the same implacable logic. I had asked for the basin and applied cold compresses to him, stroking his back and speaking gently; in spite of that, terror was overcoming him, his features contorted, I repeated my reassuring words with a smile, his eyes remained open but I had no way of judging if he saw anything, I didn't know if he had awakened or if he was still sleeping and dreaming out loud, incorporating my words into his dream, I didn't want to startle him, I kept wetting his forehead and his head and trying to bring him back to reason, to the reality of the room where we were. Slowly, the flood of words slowed down, the phrases spaced out; finally, the child closed his eyes and his wet head fell against my chest, where I held it in my palm, which seemed immense next to his little face. With a towel someone gave me, I dried his hair, then lay him down in the bed, before lying next to him without even taking off my shoes. Pacified, he breathed with a whistling but regular noise, his eyelids, swollen and translucent, quivering over his eyes. I put my arm around him and stayed for a long time next to him. Much later, the child was deep in a regular sleep and I got up: "You, stay with him," I said to the first person I met in the hallway. The others had scattered throughout the house, I glimpsed one or another of them through a half-opened door or at the end of a hallway; it was all the same to me, I returned to pick up my extinguished cigar and, relighting it, sat down beneath the portrait of the girl with the peach, opening the newspaper lying there to study the latest declarations of the foreign leader who was threatening us in such an incomprehensible manner.

At breakfast, the people gathered around the table seemed even less substantial, even more ephemeral than the day before. The woman who had spent the night with me twirled a teaspoon in a soft-boiled egg, without raising her eyes to me; her body, under a batiste robe, must have kept some traces of our nighttime games; it may have been she who had held out the light for me at the previous night's dinner, but I couldn't be sure. The children were silent and swallowed buttered toast and glasses of fruit juice; for my part, I leafed through the morning paper, full of still more unsettling news on which I found it hard to concentrate, so much did the feeling of my own presence distract me: I felt so solid that my joints ached. The doctor was announced: I joined him in the hallway and in a few words filled him in on the night's events. "There's nothing to worry about," he affirmed, "it happens at that age, with strong fevers. The main thing is to bring the temperature down, as you've rightly done." In the bedroom, he examined the child, who submitted with a tired air, without protesting; the doctor tried to ask him some questions, but he didn't remember anything. The fever had diminished. "He should eat a little," the doctor decreed, putting his instruments back in his bag. "Broth, stewed fruit, a little white rice if he can." Outside, it was still raining, and I took the large brown umbrella to escort him to his car, stepping aside to let him pass through the gate in front of me while protecting him from the rain. Alone in the street, with my back to the gate, I hesitated: what if I returned to the apartment? I looked at the street in that direction and my throat tightened when I glimpsed the two men in black, each armed with an umbrella. They held them very high up, which allowed me to see with a growing fear their shining, lifeless eyes, and their lips open in wide predatory smiles. With calm, even, resolute steps, they advanced toward me.

An Old Story

I

My head broke the surface and my mouth opened to gulp air just as, amidst loud splashing, my hands found the edge, took hold and, transferring the force of my momentum to my shoulders, hoisted my dripping body out of the water. I stood for a minute balanced on the edge, disoriented by the muted echoes of the shouts and water noises, dazzled by the fragmented sight of parts of my body in the long mirrors surrounding the pool. Around my feet, a puddle was slowly growing; a child shot by in front of me, almost making me topple backwards. I caught hold of myself, took off my cap and goggles, and, throwing a last look over my shoulder at the gleaming line of my lats, went out through the swinging doors. Dried off, clothed in a grey, silky tracksuit, pleasant to the skin, I found myself back in the hallway. I unhesitatingly passed an intersection, then another, it was rather dark here and you could barely make out the walls in the indistinct lighting; I began to run, in short strides, as if I were jogging.

The dull-colored walls streamed by; occasionally, I seemed to glimpse an opening, or at least a darker part, I couldn't really be sure, sometimes also the cloth of my jacket brushed against the wall, so that I swerved to the middle of the corridor, which must have been curving, but very slightly, almost imperceptibly, just enough to throw my running off-balance; already I was sweating, even though it was neither warm nor cold, I was breathing regularly, inhaling an insipid gulp of air every three steps and then exhaling it almost in a whistle, elbows held close to my body so as not to bump into the walls, which sometimes seemed to grow farther away and sometimes to get closer, as if the corridor were snaking back and forth. In front I could make out nothing, I moved forward almost at random, above my head I could see no ceiling, perhaps I was already running out in the open, perhaps not. A sharp shock on my elbow made me stumble, I rubbed it reflexively and turned around: an object on the wall stood out from the greyness, gleaming. I put my hand on it; it was a door handle, I leaned on it and the door opened, dragging me with it. I found myself in a familiar garden, quiet and peaceful: the sun was shining, spots of light were scattered over the mingled leaves of the ivy and the bougainvillea, neatly trimmed on their trellis; further away, the twisted trunks of old wisteria emerged from the ground to cover with their greenery the tall façade of the house, raised in front of me like a tower. It was hot and I wiped the sweat beading on my face with my sleeve. Then I went in. In the back of the hallway, through a half-opened door, a series of curious sounds reached me, low-sounding plosives interspersed with whistles: the child must have been playing war, knocking his tin soldiers over one after the other in a deluge of shots and explosions. I left him there without disturbing him and headed for the spiral staircase leading upstairs, pausing on the landing to contemplate the ironic gaze, lost in the void, of the large reproduction of the *Lady with an Ermine* hanging there. The woman was in the kitchen; at the sound of my steps she put down her knife, turned around with a smile, and came over to kiss me tenderly as she pressed against me. She was wearing a pearl-grey house dress, thin and light; I caressed her hip through the cloth, then plunged my face into her Venetian blond hair, done up in an artfully disheveled bun, to breathe in her smell of heather, moss, and almond. She laughed quietly and disengaged herself from my embrace. "I'm making dinner. It's going to take a while." She brushed my face with the tip of her fingers. "The little one's playing."—"Yes, I know. I heard him when I came in."—"Could you put him in the bath?"— "Of course. You had a good day?"—"Yes. I got the photos, they're upstairs on the dresser. Oh, another thing: we have a problem with the electrical circuit. The neighbor called."— "What did she say?"—"Apparently there are voltage spikes, it's causing power outages at their house." My face darkened. "She's out of her mind. I had our circuit overhauled twice. By a professional electrician."—"Yes, I know." I turned my back to her and went back downstairs. The sounds of battle had ceased. Before opening the door, I went into the adjoining bathroom to run the bath, checking the temperature to make sure it wasn't too hot. Then I went into the child's room. He was only wearing a t-shirt; his buttocks bare, he was squatting and photographing with a little digital camera the tin cavalrymen armed with lances and rifles, carefully lined up on the rug spread over the grey tiles. I watched him for a minute, as if through a glass wall. Then I came forward and tapped his buttocks: "Come on, it's bath time." He dropped the camera and threw himself in my arms, squealing. I lifted him up and carried him to the bathroom, where I took off his t-shirt and put him in the water. Immediately, he began slapping the surface with his hands, splashing the walls and laughing. I laughed with him but at the same time drew back, leaning on the door to watch him as he plunged completely underwater.

At the meal, the child, seated between us, chattered on about his battles. I listened to him absent-mindedly, savoring the cool wine and the langoustines sautéed in garlic. The woman, her thin face framed by blond locks that had escaped from her bun, smiled and drank as well. The child finally fell silent to attack a langoustine, trying to break one of its claws between his little baby teeth; I wiped myself with my napkin and, with the tip of my fingers, stroked his hair, blond like his mother's. His meal over, he quickly cleared his dishes and ran down the stairs, rubbing his greasy fingers on his pajamas as his mother gently scolded him. I finished clearing up as she went downstairs to put him to bed and carefully washed my hands before returning to finish my wine. A disk case was lying on the stereo, a recent recording of *Don Giovanni*; I put the third disk on and sat down in front of the bay window, lighting a thin cigar and contemplating the saffron light of evening dotting the green masses of the garden. The Commendatore was about to turn up for dinner and I thought about the meaning of this threatening, moralizing figure. He demanded, above all, to impose his law on the rebel son; but hadn't the latter run him through in the beginning of the first act? Obviously, that hadn't done any good, since now he was returning, even more monumental and deadly, the ruin of all pleasures. But the end was approaching and the son was resisting every inch of the way, like a stubborn kid, crafty and obstinate, refusing all adherence to that dead, outdated, stifling law, even if his life depended on it. Outside night was falling and I got up to turn on, one by one, the living room lamps. Then I poured myself another glass. Already the disk was coming to an end, in a comic final ensemble which sounded like the last echo of the unrelenting rascal's mocking laughter. Later on, the woman came back up, and I followed her upstairs. Her hips swayed gently in the half-light of the stairway. As she showered I quickly went through the photographs on the chest of drawers: they all showed me in the company of the child, at different times and in different situations, at the circus, at the beach, on a boat. None of them caught my eye and I left them there before getting undressed, absent-mindedly examining my lean muscles in the tall upright mirror that stood next to the door. Seen from the back, my body seemed almost feminine to me, I examined the ass, white and round like the woman's. When she emerged from the bathroom, naked and still wet, her long hair rolled up in a towel, I pulled her by the shoulders and pushed her onto the bedspread, a thick golden cloth embroidered with long green grass. She fell on her stomach with a little cry and I reached out to turn off the light. Now only the pale gleam of the moon lit the room, it flowed through the windows behind which stood out the mad twists of the wisteria, illuminating the green leaves of the embroidery and the white body sprawled out on it, the long, thin back, the hips, the twin globes of the buttocks. I lay down on top of this body and it shivered. The towel had fallen away and the hair covered her face. With the tips of my feet, I spread her legs, I slipped a hand beneath her belly to raise her hips, and pressed my erect member against her sex. But it was dry, I withdrew a little, poured saliva on my fingers and smeared the opening, gently massaging it. Then I could enter easily. Her breathing accelerated, her behind, beneath me, began moving, her long body, held in both my hands, went taut and a cry escaped her, immediately broken off. I felt myself melting with sweetness, a long needle of delight pierced my back, very thin, stretching the skin on the back of my neck and electrifying it. I turned my head: in the mirror, pale under the moonlight, I could again see my ass and the top of my sinewy thighs, hers too, pinned beneath, and in between them dark, reddish, indistinct shapes. Fascinated by this incongruous spectacle, I slowed down, the woman, her body lost in the long embroidered grass leaves of the bedspread, was panting, her hand sought my hip, I could see it in the mirror, the lacquered nails embedded in my muscles, while next to the mirror the door opened and in the section of moonlight I saw the pointy little face of the child, his eyes wide open and his lips stubborn, obstinate. I froze. The face also remained motionless; next to it, I could still see in the mirror the double mass of buttocks and the dark jumble of organs between them. I could feel the pleasure mounting, the woman was moaning, I withdrew abruptly and rolled onto my side, my wet, scarlet member still throbbing, I was coming in long spurts almost without realizing it, the kid's face had disappeared into the darkness of the stairway, we could hear his little bare feet hurriedly slapping the stone steps, the woman was looking at me with a lost, confused air, I was still coming. Dripping with sweat, my breathing irregular, I rolled completely onto my back and distractedly wiped my stomach with the sheet as the woman, already standing, put on a bathrobe to go follow the child.

I must have been sleeping by the time she came back to bed. When I woke up, the sky through the windows was growing pale. The tentacles of the wisteria waved gently; the birds nestling in the branches began singing, a concert of shrill chirps. The woman lay half turned away, her face once again hidden beneath her long loose hair, I left her and quickly slipped into my tracksuit before going down to the living room. I entertained the idea of making myself coffee, immediately decided against it, and went down to the lower floor where the boy, curled in a narrow wooden bed, was sleeping. I sat on the edge and contemplated his severe face, lit by the slanting dawn light. Here too, birdsong filled the room. The child seemed to be breathing with difficulty, sweat was sticking his blond hair to his forehead, I brushed it away and he opened his eyes. "You are going?" he said without moving. I nodded. "I don't want you to," he said, staring at me stubbornly, almost greedily.—"But I have to," I answered in a low voice.—"Why?" I thought about that and then replied: "Because I want to." His gaze, both powerless and obstinate, grew veiled: "So, when you're happy, I'm unhappy. And when I'm happy, you're unhappy."—"No, that's not it at all. You're getting it all mixed up." I bent over, delicately kissed his

damp forehead, got up and went out. In the garden, everything was calm, the leaves rustled gently, hiding the abrupt
movements of the birds, which still hadn't fallen silent. It was
already hot, a strong morning heat that clung to the skin. The
door opened easily and I found the hallway where I resumed
my deliberate running, the wide strides in rhythm with my
breathing. The hallway appeared a little lighter, I seemed
better able to perceive the curves, even if I couldn't manage
precisely to locate either the walls or the ceiling, if there even
was one. The temperature, here, was more moderate, but my
body, heated by the running, was sweating in my clothes;
the pants stuck to my hips, which didn't prevent me, like a
well-oiled machine, from maintaining a regular rhythm. I
passed dark openings without slowing down, junctions or
possibly merely alcoves; finally something on my left drew
my attention, a metallic brilliance that floated in the corner
of my vision; without hesitating or slowing down, I found
the handle, opened the door and crossed the threshold. My
foot sank into something soft and I stopped short. I found
myself in a rather large, semi-dark room, sparsely furnished;
on the walls, the golden vines of the wallpaper intertwined
as they climbed; a dark red, almost blood-colored carpet covered the floor. Across the room, beyond the bed covered in
a heavy golden cloth embroidered with long green grass, a
figure with close-cropped jet black hair was standing in front
of the window; the shutters were closed, but it was staring
at something in the window, its own reflection perhaps. I
contemplated it for a minute as if through a window pane,
with a light, almost joyful feeling. At the sound of the door
closing, it turned around, and I saw then that it was a woman,

a beautiful woman whose matte, sharp-featured face lit up with a smile when she saw me. She skirted round the bed and embraced me, pressing her mobile little tongue between my lips, laughing. I lost my balance and fell with her onto the green leaves of the bedspread, my nose pressed against her short hair, filling my face with the smell of earth and cinnamon. Beneath me, she twisted, laughing, and tried to break loose. I straightened up and undertook as best I could to unbutton her sheer tulle blouse, brushing against her breasts held in by a rigid bra. She laughed again and slipped between my hands before kneeling on the green and gold expanse of the bed to re-button her blouse. "In the street," she said, lifting her beautiful dark eyes, full of cheerfulness beneath eyelashes heavy with mascara, "I imagined I was touching your face. And now, here you are." I stretched my hand out again toward her body and she brushed it away, laughing: "What impatience! Wait, I'm dying of hunger." She picked up the receiver next to the bed, dialed a number and, holding up a cardboard menu, named a few items. I rose and shook my numb legs, then went into the bathroom where I opened wide the heavy porcelain faucets of the bathtub, my fingers beneath the stream of water to gauge the temperature.

In the water, her back to me, she leaned her long brown body against mine. Her short, thick hair tickled my nostrils; I patiently caressed her arms, her belly, the tops of her breasts floating on the surface of the slightly greenish bathwater. A number of little scars decorated her dusky skin, rather thick, the bumps long or short depending on the place, I counted three on her left shoulder, one on her groin, a large one on her ribs, just beneath the right breast, another forked one at the angle of her jaw. Abrupt knocks sounded on the door to the room. The girl turned round in a loud splash, placed a quick kiss on my lips, and leapt out of the bathtub, slipping her streaming body into a terrycloth bathrobe before going to the door. I relaxed in the water, my face scarcely showing above the surface. A powerful feeling of plenitude filled my body, but an almost unsettling plenitude, impossible to grasp or possess, which left something like a sensation of emptiness behind it. Some noises, stifled by the water covering my ears, reached me indistinctly. I got out of the bath, dried myself quickly, pulled on the other bathrobe hanging there and, without taking the trouble to close it, went back into the bedroom. Kneeling once again on the golden bedspread, the girl was contemplating a large tray on which were lined up dishes in lacquered wood, covered with raw fish and pickled vegetables. Two golden beers frothed in tapered glasses. I joined her and began eating without a word. Aside from the sound of the chopsticks everything was quiet; behind the shutters, where there must have been a street or a courtyard, there was not a sound; a lone lamp standing by the bedside lit us with its yellowish halo, and I could distinctly make out our reflections in the windowpanes, two slightly blurred silhouettes, draped in white, which stood out from the field of green grasses of the bedspread. From time to time one of us offered a piece of fish to the other, who snapped it up with a surprised smile; when I kissed her, her lips had the bitter taste of beer. It was very dry in this room, I could feel my skin pulling at my hands and face; the raw fish as well made me thirsty, I quickly finished my beer. The girl got up, took my empty glass, and went into the bathroom. I finished the last little vegetables and piled the plates on the tray to go put it in a corner, on the floor. The girl still hadn't come out and I got rid of my bathrobe to stretch out on the bedspread, on my belly, my head resting on my crossed arms. Turning my face I could glimpse the twin moon of my buttocks reflected in one of the windowpanes, white and slightly rounded. When the young woman reappeared she was naked too, splendid, her bare feet advanced on the blood-red carpet as she held the glass filled with water in front of her, her hips caught in a leather harness that held a long black phallus strapped to her pubis. I took the glass from her hand and drank. She moved behind me, without thinking I spread my legs and pointed my toes, her fingers, smeared with a liquid, slippery substance, threaded their way between my buttocks to massage the areola of my anus, my hips rose, she lay on top of me and I heard her husky breathing whistling in my ear as her hand played with my hair, pressing my head onto the bedspread. The object attached to her hips beat against my ass, heavy, hard, and silky. I arched my hips a little and it began to move between my buttocks, with a very deliberate slowness, then it withdrew and the tip caught, I slipped a hand behind my back to guide it and the girl leaned in with all her weight: then my ass opened all of a sudden and she entered me, her hands gripping my buttocks to spread them more and her head weighing on my neck. A cold, biting flame filled my pelvis, I hollowed out my back some more and leaned with both hands against the headboard, her hips were beating against mine now in large long strokes that kept spreading further through my body horribly sweet sensations, my legs twisted, sought a support, slid, her firm, soft thighs pressed on mine, her hands, now, rose up and pressed with all their weight on my head. Pleasure invaded my neck and shoulders, a long, diffuse, electric stream, I arched my back convulsively, my member, limp and almost forgotten, beat against the embroidery of the cloth to the rhythm of her moving hips; supporting myself on one shoulder, I pulled back a little, turned onto my side and opened my eyes to look beneath her arm. Her brown thigh, marked with several scars, entwined my own, much paler and covered with curly hairs; the leather straps which held in place the object with which she was working my hips shaped small bulges in her flesh: and in the window, beyond her long slim back, I could see her ass, two golden orbs pushed upwards by the straps beneath them, overlapping mine on the green and golden field of the bedspread. All of a sudden, the light went out, erasing the image in the window and plunging the room into darkness; even with my eyes wide open I could see nothing, the electricity must have gone out, I was coming now with all my muscles and she, heaving against me and panting, must have been coming too, finally she collapsed on my back, her pelvis tense against my buttocks, the immobile phallus planted inside me, I slipped one hand behind my head to rub her hair, she bit my neck and I still spasmodically moved my hips. The blade of pleasure, long successive waves, kept unfurling throughout my abandoned body. I wanted to pull myself together, perhaps withdraw to take her in turn, but a great somnolence invaded me, I yawned, my hands moved with more and more languor and lightness, I ran my fingers again over my back, my hips and her thighs and I fell asleep thus, her member still inside me and her body stretched out on mine, melting with pleasure.

The return of the electricity woke me up. The girl had rolled onto her side, her legs intertwined with mine, the phallus still lodged inside me. Spreading apart my buttocks, I slowly pulled away, it was dry now and it stuck a little; finally the object came out and fell onto the bedspread with a small dull thud. My mouth was dry and pasty; I carefully disentangled myself from her legs, rose up and headed to the bathroom. The white light of the neon dazzled me, I turned it off right away; still blinking, I leaned over the sink to drink greedily from the faucet. When I came back out I contemplated the young woman: she was still sleeping, stretched out on her side, the phallus almost completely hidden in the shadow of her curved body; behind her, the yellow light of the bedside lamp illuminated her naked, brown back, the long green grasses of the bedspread crumpled beneath her body, the gilt vines of the wallpaper. I sat next to her and lightly ran the flat of my fingertips over the nape of her neck, her spine, her buttocks. She shivered but didn't wake up. Her skin, almost rough, grated beneath my fingers; between her legs, the secretions had dried on the black phallus, reflecting light in places. I should turn down the heat, I thought confusedly. But I could see no thermostat, no temperature control. I got back up, filled two glasses of water, and placed them on the radiator; then I turned off the light and lay down again alongside the girl, on my belly, one hand on the small of her back. Sounds of water emanating from the bathroom woke me completely. The light was on again and I was alone on the bed. I got up, knocked on the door to the bathroom, and went in without waiting for a reply: the girl, sitting naked on the toilet, her elbows resting on her knees, the phallus still fixed to her belly, was peeing. I bent over to kiss her hair. She wiped herself and got up in a swift movement that made her artificial member bounce, before pressing the flush handle. "Aren't you going to take that off?" I asked her as she rinsed her face and ran wet fingers through her hair. "Why? I like having a cock. I think I'll wear it all day." She laughed and I went out to stretch out on the bed. It was still just as hot and dry and I was thirsty again. She came out behind me as the little musical tone of a cellphone rang out. "Oh! I have to go," she said cheerfully as she examined the screen. Leaning on one elbow, I watched her get dressed. She struggled with her jeans, already almost too narrow for her hips, trying to fit the object lying next to her thigh into them. Finally she managed to zipper them and buckle her belt. Then she put on her bra and her blouse, before tapping the bulge in her jeans: "Nice package, don't you think?" I reached out and stroked it without a word. She laughed, shook her head, and went out. I got up, showered quickly, and got dressed. The smooth, silky material of the tracksuit glided pleasantly on my skin. At the entrance to the bedroom, I hesitated: there were two doors, one opposite the other, something I hadn't noticed before. Which one had the girl taken? It didn't matter. I opened one at random and crossed the threshold with a confident step; already my feet, in sneakers light as feathers, found their short stride again; I brought my elbows in against my ribs and concentrated on my breathing, inhaling through my mouth to the rhythm of my steps. The air here was less dry than in the bedroom, sweat soon beaded on my face, soaked my armpits, the hollow of my back; I followed the curve of the grey hallway, advancing almost noiselessly. It was dark, but that didn't bother me too much, I could still see well enough; I could not, however, make out any source of light, the walls seemed smooth, identical, indistinct, I wondered vaguely where the lighting could be coming from, while still aware that it was of no importance. Here and there, a darker area seemed to open onto a cubbyhole, or even a tunnel, I went on my way without slowing down, following the curve that continued on, and like a child I held out my hand and let my fingers trail along the wall until they came up against an object that I hadn't seen. It was a doorknob, I pushed it and opened the door. Right away, I knew that this space suited me. It was a vast and very bright studio, its walls covered with books; in the back a long bay window overlooked piles of little buildings rising in levels in front of a grey, luminous strip of sea. I came over and rested my hands on the long table in front of the window as I examined the city, contemplating the changing colors of the façades as the light faded. Then I turned around. A disk case was lying on a stereo, old recordings of Mozart piano concertos; I put one on at random and strolled through the studio listening to the first notes, letting my gaze wander absent-mindedly over the bindings of the books and the many engravings and reproductions hanging between the bookcases. The cheerful, lucid notes of the music danced through the room, filling me with a profound feeling of serene lightness. I poured myself a glass of schnapps, lit a little cigar found in a box, and burrowed into a black leather sofa to leaf through an album lying there, on a coffee table. In oblong format, bound in white cloth, it showed a series of photographs of naked men and women, executing various movements broken down into stop motion sequences by a multiple camera setup. I paused at one plate: a man, with a powerful movement, was drawing another man around his body to throw him on the ground, face-down, before falling on top of him to pin him there, his head seemingly confused with that of his opponent as the twin white globes of the buttocks and the vigorous lines of the thighs overlapped each other, a sinuous heap of forms, forever fixed in place by the successive shutter releases.

It was cool in this studio, almost cold. I changed the disk for another and searched through the cupboards for something to eat. There wasn't much, but I was able to throw together a refreshing meal of sardines in oil, raw onions, black bread, and rosé. As I was finishing it my body shivered with cold; I quickly cleared the dishes and went to run the shower, waiting for the water to get hot before undressing and plunging myself underneath it. In the water I stretched my muscles, enjoying the sensations provoked by this long, wiry body. In the bedroom, I dried myself in front of a large round mirror placed at the foot of the bed, a simple mattress resting on the ground covered with a thick embroidered bedspread, long green grass on a golden background. The mirror showed only the lower part of my body, which, despite the little member shrunken against the balls, seemed almost like a womanish body to me, an image that caused me no anxiety but rather a diffuse, caressing feeling of pleasure. I turned around to contemplate from the side the curve of the thigh, the arch of the hips, the delicate oval of the buttock. I knelt down on the bed, my back to the mirror, and turned my head. The ass, hiding the top of the body, was now facing the circle of the mirror, and I spread it slightly with one hand, revealing the yellowish flower of the anus that blinked quietly, as if it were gazing at itself, a tiny opening but bottomless, dazzling. I found that very beautiful and I contemplated it for a long time before finally relaxing and stretching out full-length on the bedspread. I was no longer cold and I fell asleep that way, as if I were lying on a field of grass, rocked by the light-hearted, mocking, playful cadences of a last concerto. When I woke up it was dark, everything was quiet, goosebumps covered my skin and I slipped beneath the bedspread and sheets, pulling them around me to get warm. But I couldn't fall back asleep and finally I got up, the bedspread still draped around my shoulders, to go drink a glass of water in the kitchenette. Through the bay window, down below, I could see in the darkness a lozenge of light, the window of a neighboring apartment forming a section crossed lengthwise by a long sofa upholstered in white upon which had sunk a young woman in delicate underclothes. A small round mirror was hanging above the sofa and she was putting on makeup, kneeling before it, her back arched a little to keep her balance. From time to time, she raised her arm to adjust the angle of the mirror, which was attached to a mobile support, or else to bring it closer to her face, and this gesture stretched her breast nestled in an underwire bra and made the edge of her pectoral muscle bulge, like a milky white cable attached to her shoulder. She carried out these gestures with swift precision, absorbed in the unconscious happiness of this routine so familiar to her body. I watched her for a while and then went back to bed. Sleep quickly brought me to the entrance of a house, a house that must have been my own, locked after a long absence. A series of doors led to the kitchen, out of which rushed a black cat as soon as I opened the door. The room stank of shit and trash, the cat must have been locked up in it during my entire absence and had soiled everything: No matter, I said to myself, shrugging my shoulders, my wife will clean it. I opened the door that led to the small back garden to air it out, then went down to the cellar; there I crossed a long hallway that led to a kind of grotto, opening onto the large front garden. My workers were waiting there. "So, Emilio," I said, "how's the work going?" The man I had spoken to came forward, hat in hand, and gestured for me to follow him outside. The view that greeted me filled me with horror: the garden, which had previously formed beautiful undulating curves protected from the neighbors' sight, was now completely filled in, forming a flat surface at the same level as the next house. Distraught, I looked around me: the old ruined barn adjoining the house had disappeared; Emilio, in an excess of zeal, must have had it torn down to fill in the garden. Beside myself, I yelled at him violently: "But Emilio! This is not at all what I asked you to do!" Emilio timidly tried to defend himself as I ran back and forth, noting the extent of the damage. The garden thus renovated ended up at the windows of the neighboring house, barely hidden by a few shrubs, and now extended a small byroad that used to end at the outskirts of my property. In fact, a car was coming down and crossing my garden, cheerfully honking as it passed. "Come on, Emilio!" I shouted. "Just look at this! And what about my barn? Who gave you the order to demolish it?" In vain, I thought about how all this could be repaired, but the damages were too great, it seemed an impossible task. The car emerged from the garden by an open gate next to the neighbors' house, and I followed it, still foaming. "Well now, first of all, close all this up!" I barked, pointing at the road. "This is a private property here, good God, not a highway!" I went out and contemplated the street. Another car was now coming slowly toward me, driven by a blond woman. Emilio had come out as well and was standing next to me, a little behind me. The car slowed down, as if to park, but didn't stop and slowly crashed with a great crunch of sheet metal against the stone pillar that supported the gate. I rushed forward but the driver, who was still holding onto the driving wheel with both hands, wasn't hurt. I thought I recognized my neighbor, who, what's more curious, resembled my wife as well as my mother—two women who also didn't know how to drive —and I went over to talk with her about our new problem of proximity; but she didn't even let me open my mouth before pouring out a litany of complaints through the lowered window: "Oh, you! Do you know that your electric circuit is completely out of whack? There are surges all the time, they're causing outages in the neighborhood." These words filled me with fury and I began shouting as well: "Madam, you're exaggerating! I've had that circuit completely overhauled by a professional electrician, twice in a row. That's enough, now!" When I woke up a cold light was falling in the room, making the golden field of the bedspread sparkle, but warming nothing. I got up and quickly got dressed, swallowed a glass of juice, and went out. In the hallway I resumed my running without hesitation; the effort warmed me up and helped me shed the last scraps of sleep. In my distraction, however, I bumped several times against the walls, the indistinct light blurred all details and I couldn't always place them with precision; sometimes darker zones appeared, junctions perhaps or else some nook, I avoided them and tried to stay in the center of the hallway, moving with short regular strides, my sneakers falling with a muted sound on a ground as smooth as the walls. I breathed evenly, in short quick puffs; I didn't get tired, I knew I could run a long time this way. At one moment, I noticed that my shoelace had come untied, and I interrupted my running to kneel down and re-tie it; when I raised my head, I noticed that I was in front of a door handle, I leaned on it without hesitating and a door opened, which I went through as I straightened up. A few steps further in, there waited a proud, beautiful, rather curvaceous woman. She was standing with one hand on her hip; the other was bringing a long cigarette holder to her lips, painted blood-red: "You're late, darling," she murmured, exhaling a puff of smoke and taking me by the hand. "Good Lord, you're sweating. And you're not even dressed." Golden bracelets jingled on her wrist; I leaned over and brushed my lips against her bare shoulder, my nose buried in her long reddish curls, inhaling their rich, almost musky smell of amber. "Forgive me. I had to run."—"That's all right. Come." I followed her through a large room, at the back of which a sliding glass door, open, led outside. A brilliant green lawn, over which two yapping Dalmatians were chasing each other, stretched out to copses of palm trees, ficus, and bougainvillea; a group of girls in tight-fitting shorts and tank tops or bras were playing volleyball. "Almost everyone is here already," my friend said in a slight tone of reproach as she climbed a stone staircase that ran alongside the façade of the house. Her stiletto heels clicked on the stone and her hips swayed in front of me. The staircase led to a vast, tiled terrace the color of terra cotta, in the center of which shone the emerald-green water of a long rectangular pool. A tall girl with black hair cut short, topless, was doing laps; near the edge, another young woman with an artfully disheveled Venetian blond bun, stretched out on her belly and leaning on her elbows, was following my movements with a mocking gaze; her pretty little feet, with bright red nails, swayed above her well-rounded buttocks, enclosed in a white swimsuit with blue stripes that left her slim back bare. I contemplated this magnificent body with a pang of envy; but already my friend was leading me through another sliding glass door into a vast living room, its carpet and walls a pale grey, with burnt orange and lemon yellow drapes, arranged on several different levels and furnished with elegance and restraint in green tones that went with the lawn. In the center rose a sort of bed or sofa without a back, of imposing dimensions, covered with a thick golden cloth embroidered with long green grass. We skirted around the piece of furniture and followed a long hallway that led to a bedroom. The adjoining bathroom, tiled in white with a polished slate floor, seemed immense. "Shower there," my friend ordered. "I'll find something for you to wear. Something classic, no?" She ran her painted nails over my chin: "And shave. You're stubbly." I quickly undressed and did what she had ordered. I had just finished shaving when she returned with a pile of clothes that she placed on a chair. It took some time to try them on, the sizes weren't always right; she handed me a grey lace bra whose underwire rounded my form a little, a skin-tight pair of panties in embroidered tulle, and some silk stockings surmounted with a wide band of lace, also grey but of a darker shade, almost metallic. Perched on high pumps into which I had slipped my feet, I admired in the mirror the curve of my buttocks and thighs set off by the lace, delaying putting on the dress. It was sublime, a long body-skimming sheath made of pearl grey linen and rayon knit to form a fine silky jersey, without the slightest seam, and lined inside with a pale pink silk that flowed delicately on my skin as I slipped it over my head. The shoulder straps left my angular shoulders bare; in front, the cloth, molded by the bra, gave me a tiny but charming chest. My friend smoothed the cloth over my hips, without taking her eyes off our reflection in the mirror. Then she made me up, blue-grey for my eyelids, a pinkish shade for my lips, and a darker pink tint for my nails; she also put some jewelry on me, pearl earrings, a woven choker, a few tastefully wrought silver rings and bracelets. For my hair, it was simple: she smoothed it with gel, then separated it into a long side part, with a lock lying flat across my forehead and the sides held back with hair-pins. I balanced on my heels and made a few movements. "You are superb," my friend whispered hoarsely at the tall woman with a regal bearing whose gaze was devouring me from the mirror, her eyes enlarged by eyeliner and mascara, blazing with excitation. "I might not be the greatest beauty of the evening," I murmured, pivoting on my heels and gazing over my shoulder at the back and hips of the figure in the mirror, "but my ass will make more than a few of the girls hard."

The party was in full swing. The whirlwind of women all around me gave me a slight vertigo; noise echoed in my ears, music, laughter, shouts, clinking of glasses and jewelry; I found myself in the middle of a slow ballet of winks, pouts, smiles, light touches, caressing gestures, fragments of movements multiplied in the long mirrors framing the living room. The narrow dress forced me to take tiny steps, and I was still ill at ease on my high heels; but little by little I found my balance, and with it I gained more self-confidence and began to laugh, talk, gesticulate, as freely as my companions. My friend handed me a cocktail, a gin and tonic, cool, sparkling, almost bitter, and leaned over to breathe a few words into my ear: "Everything is perfect here, isn't it? We're amongst ourselves." There was too much noise to make myself heard, so I nodded. On a slightly elevated part of the room, three girls were dancing, swaying their hips, their pretty behinds shapely in miniskirts or shorts, their legs long and bare and smooth. Quite close to me, a haughty woman with a sculptural, exaggerated body, almost a head taller than me, was staring fixedly at herself in a mirror, her hands running up her hips and belly to gravely weigh her bulging breasts. The young woman with the blond hair in a bun whom I had seen earlier by the pool in a striped swimsuit had joined us, dressed now in a short embroidered dress with a violet stole draped over her narrow shoulders. Her hand rested familiarly on the hollow of my back and she brushed my neck with her lips: "What a beautiful dress! It suits you." I blushed with pleasure and, pulling her neck toward me, pressed my mouth against hers. Near us, my friend was laughing; in the mirror in front of me, I could see the young woman's back and hips, our intertwined bodies, my own gaze filtered through her loose strands of hair which smelled of heather, moss, and almond. Finally she broke away and contemplated me with a brief, joyful smile; then, stroking my face with the tips of her fingers, she moved away: "See you soon." I sipped my drink as I watched her disappear into the crowd. My friend was still laughing and handed me a lipstick: poised in front of the mirror, I carefully retouched the outline of my lips; rolling one against the other in that so intimately feminine gesture, spreading a sensual joy through my entire body. Near me several girls were kissing now, standing against the walls or on the sofas, I could see hands with colorful nails wandering over thighs and buttocks and disappearing beneath dresses or skirts; breasts began appearing, well-rounded, the nipples erect and calling for lips; the girl with the short hair who had been doing laps in the pool was kneeling now between the thighs of the tall sculptural woman; and she, above the head pressing in on her, was still staring at herself in the mirror. I turned toward her reflection and tried to meet her gaze but it remained riveted on itself, impenetrable, and thus I could contemplate her at my leisure, without her noticing; seen from this angle her face took on a hard, angular, almost masculine aspect, her gaze, as the head with the thick close-cropped black hair moved down the length of her body, darkened, took on a fierce, wild look; and when finally the girl, with both hands, parted her thighs to place her beautiful painted mouth on her sex, her eyes came alive with a furious, devouring, superb joy. I kept sipping my drink without taking my eyes off the spectacle in the mirror; my friend was watching the couple itself over my shoulder and I could also see, in front of my own, the reflection of her ample curves and curly hair. A little silver tray that had been circulating among the guests reached us; I leaned over, delicately grasped the glass straw, and inhaled a line of white powder, followed by another; a shiver traveled through my body, I straightened up, arched nervously on my legs perched on the high heels, and with one hand smoothed the knit cloth over my hip and buttock. My friend took some cocaine as well and I helped her hold the tray. Then I passed it on to another woman and took my friend by the hand to lead her outside. As I crossed the threshold of the sliding glass door I shivered, it was cold outside the house, humid too, the grass, beneath the light of lamps placed all over, shone with dew. "There's a lot of light," I said to my friend. "Are you sure the fuses won't blow?"—"Don't worry about it. We had the entire circuit overhauled twice, by a professional electrician." Here too there were dozens of guests, talking or kissing while drinking, laughing, smoking. Several girls, naked except for thongs or bathing suits, were swimming in the illuminated water of the pool, their beautiful, slim bodies deformed by the waves of green water. On the edge, kneeling, naked too, apart from a thin pair of black and purple lace panties, the young woman with the half undone bun whom I had kissed was scrutinizing her image in the lapping water. From where I stood, I could see her profile: her long neck freed by the bun, her sharp shoulder, the gracious curve of her back were almost those of a boy; but the round shape of her hips, when she straightened up in a fluid motion, the long firm buttocks that stretched the translucent cloth of the panties, were indeed those of a woman, a real woman. I was still drinking, my friend had handed me another gin and tonic and my lipstick stained the rim of the glass, I could feel my skin bristling in its underclothes, seeking with delight, in the places where it remained bare, silky contact with the pink lining of the dress. The young blond woman, hands on her knees and buttocks arched behind her like a little girl, was still contemplating herself in the pool water, and this spectacle filled me with joy. Then all of a sudden she stood up, arms raised and tiny breasts jutting out, took a deep breath, and dove in, erasing her reflection. I watched the long white body flow underwater, arms down by its sides, propelled by the feet. My friend was stroking my hips and my buttocks, making the almost liquid jersey of the dress slide over the rougher cloth of the lining, but I barely noticed. "You like her," her voice spoke in my ear. "More than me."—"It's not that," I said sadly. "I'm jealous of her body. Mine will never be like that."—"You are very beautiful, too. Your body excites me."—"Maybe. But it's not the same thing." I pressed against her, my heart beating. The girl was hauling herself out of the water, streaming, her hair undone and soaked, her wet panties taut over her delicate little parts. Another woman handed her a towel and she covered her shoulders with it before pattering toward us: "Give me something to drink!" she cried out, breaking into joyful laughter. Still leaning against my friend, who was now gently stroking my belly, I handed her my glass with an affectionate smile. I felt happy and light, my mind expanding from the alcohol and the cocaine, overwhelmed by the fullness of the ambiguous body that the beautiful clothes my friend had lent me shaped for me. "You'll catch cold," I said to the blond girl who was shivering, reaching out my fingers to wipe away the water beading on the bristling skin of her arm. "Come dry off."

Alone now in the bathroom, I examined my face in the harsh, pitiless neon light. Beneath its mask of colors and powders it looked hollow to me, almost feverish. I quickly dashed a little powder on my burning cheeks before returning to the living room. The blond girl had gone in before me and, her image multiplied in the mirrors, was dancing almost naked in front of the large green and gold covered bed. All around was a vast confusion of bodies; partially or entirely undressed, they intertwined on the sofas and the carpet, opening up to each other in a wild joyous communism where organs, hands, and greedy mouths took precedence over individuals, splitting them open, confusing them, mingling them in a tide of cries and husky sighs, shaken by irregular spasms. I looked for my friend: she was still standing beyond the sliding glass door, poised with an ironic air on her high heels and smoking a cigarette, contemplating with an indifferent gaze, through the glass, the disordered utopia of bodies in the midst of which I slowly made my way forward. Having reached the blond girl, I took her by the shoulders and lay her on her belly, settling her tiny chest and her face in the long embroidered grass of the cloth. As if unwittingly, she spread her legs; I kneeled behind her on the divan and stroked her thin, nervous thighs; when I pulled the thin cloth of her panties toward me, her buttocks arched and then relaxed and spread under the pressure of my fingers. I bent down and brushed my lips against the still bristling skin of her ass; elbows drawn up against her sides, she shivered; then I slipped my tongue into the cleft, tasting a slight bitterness at the touch of the anus, nestled amid a tiny tuft of blond hair. I slipped one hand under her narrow body, along her belly and then her groin, pushing away the wet cloth of her panties to roll her small, soft member and her shriveled balls between my fingers. She began to groan, I lapped at her anus in quick strokes while playing with her parts, my own member had grown hard and I straightened to pull up my dress and extract it from my panties, I coated it with saliva and then drew against my belly the girl's back and bare ass and slipped into her in one stroke before falling forward, my teeth on the curly hairs on the nape of her neck. The young woman, her hands clenched in the embroidered bedspread, her breath cut short, groaned in pleasure, I let go of her soft member and stroked a breast, turning a little and leaning with my other hand on her neck: thus, I could see parts of our bodies in the mirror, my ass, still molded in the jersey of the dress, drawing a pearl-grey curve highlighted by the ceiling lamp with, beneath it, almost crimson, naked except for the thin creased strip of the panties, arched on the gold and green weft of the fabric, the thigh and the ass of the blond girl. I pressed her thin little body tightly in my hands and then went back to her sex, she was hard now and the member, stiff, felt minuscule in my fingers, I jerked it off while continuing to burrow into her ass, she was panting and came quickly in a squeal, her behind and back quivering, without end. Then she sank onto the embroidered grass, expelling my member from her ass in a long, slippery motion. I hadn't come yet and my member was throbbing, I was panting like her, my hands leaning on her long white thighs. But already another body was settling against my own and I lifted my head to rub it against hers: it was the tall girl with the close-cropped hair, whose thick, black hair, pressed against my face, filled my nostrils with a smell of earth and cinnamon. I turned my head to kiss her lips: just in front of my eyes, a long forked scar barred the angle of her jaw. Completely naked, she pressed against my back, stroking my chest, spreading my thighs with her knees; then she lifted my dress high up over my hips, drew my panties down just under my buttocks and began massaging my own anus, with the pad of her thumb, wet with saliva. Behind the window, my friend, impassive, was watching us attentively; the blond girl had curled up in a ball, and, from the far side of the divan, was also watching us, her large eyes moist from pleasure. The member of the girl with the black hair was beating against my ass, heavy, warm, and soft; pressed against her body, palpitating with excitation, I could feel my own body harden, take on for a brief instant all the density of the stone of a fruit before slowly beginning to melt. With my hand behind me, my heart beating, I guided the member, slippery with saliva, to my anus, it pressed and widened me and entered, filling my entire back with joy, unfurling it beneath the cloth of the dress. I was no longer hard at all, my parts beat limply against the lace of my lowered panties, my thighs, sheathed in silk, pushed against the muscular thighs of the girl burrowing powerfully into me, I collapsed onto one shoulder, twisting a little to the side, thus I could again see framed in the mirrors parts of our bodies, a mobile mound of pale flesh and pieces of disparate clothing piled on the verdant expanse of cloth, with, at the very top, the rounded ass of the girl, quivering at each thrust, then beneath that my thigh and the curve of my buttock, outlined by the grey of the stockings and the bunched-up dress. Her hands were pressing with all their weight on my neck and head and this is how, split in two by her magnificent sex, my body tore away from itself, projecting itself like a shade over those surrounding it, the one dominating it and the others all around, blurred and dismembered by the pleasure bearing them up like a vast swell.

When I opened my eyes we were all three sprawled on the embroidered cloth, our limbs intertwined, naked apart from a few pieces of tulle and lace. My mouth was pasty, cramps racked my muscles. The young woman with the Venetian blond hair was sleeping on her belly, completely naked; the one with the black hair was sleeping on her back, her long penis lying across her thigh. I brushed against it with the backs of my fingers, but the girl didn't wake up. I rose, sat on the edge of the wide bed, and took off the pump that had remained on one foot all night, along with the silk stocking. Despite the acid pain running through my head, a great feeling of peace and plenitude filled my body. Around us, other girls were sleeping as well, scattered over the sofas and thick carpets, naked or half-clothed. Many of them had hard-ons in their sleep, one of them, a very slim little girl with a huge chest, was absent-mindedly caressing her breast and letting out little yelps. There was no sign of my friend. I got up and wandered through the silent house to find the bathroom where I urinated for a long time, seated on the toilet. Then I removed my makeup and took a shower, stretching with pleasure under the hot stream. My running clothes were still lying in the corner and I quickly slipped them on after drying myself off. In the living room, my two companions were still sleeping, snuggled against each other now in the middle of the green and gold field of the large cloth. The girl with the cropped hair had turned onto her side and their buttocks fit together, the thin, sinewy bottom of the blond girl half hidden beneath the more muscular buttocks of the other. My sneakers made no sound on the carpet and I awoke no one on my way out. I went downstairs, crossed through the house and opened the back door to pass into the hallway; as soon as I closed it, I began to run, zipping my jogging suit up to my neck. I didn't count my steps, they fell one after the other, firm and regular like my breath, I guided myself as well as I could in the indistinct light, trying to guess the curve of the hallway, anxious not to bump into a wall. From time to time, when it became too dark, I held out a hand to guide me, but sometimes my fingers found nothing but emptiness, an intersection perhaps or just a recess, I faltered but didn't stop, struggling to keep going. When my hand banged into a metallic object, I knew right away it was a doorknob, I stopped short to grasp it and opened the door. The light, beyond the threshold, dazzled me, I blinked and shielded my face with my arm. The air was like a furnace, already my face was covered with sweat, I quickly took off my jacket to wipe myself with it, before tying it around my waist. Then I looked around me. I found myself at the edge of an expanse of red earth, on which were scattered groups of round huts, with earthen walls and thatched roofs. People were coming and going, most of them women and bands of children, a few men as well, all with black skin and short, curly hair, dressed in bright colors that often clashed. A few tall palm trees rose between the huts; further on stood a vast wall of vegetation, where the brilliant green of the mango trees stood out from the darker tints, green-grey or yellowish, of the other trees. Bird sounds filled the air, children's shouts burst out; sometimes too the barking of an invisible dog resounded. The air was heavy, electric. A woman, sitting in front of a blackened pot simmering on a little fire in the shade near a hut, gestured at me with her wooden ladle to approach. Near her, on a woven straw mat, a little baby was sleeping, a naked girl with just a colored cord around her hips. The woman pointed to another stool and handed me a tin spoon and a steaming bowl filled with red beans. I was very hungry and I cheerfully devoured the dish, thanking her with a smile and a few words; she answered in a language that I did not understand, encouraging me with a gesture to keep eating. It lacked salt but that didn't matter, I swallowed spoonful after spoonful and scraped the bowl. I was still sweating copiously, the damp heat stuck my soaking clothes to my body. A gust of hot wind shook the palm trees and the woman raised her head. I looked too: heavy black clouds were covering the sky above the forest. Already the first drops were splattering the ground, throwing up particles of red dirt; the woman gathered the baby in its mat and then grasped the pot, gesticulating for me to follow her under a thatched roof erected over some posts, like a hut without walls. There were three little chairs and wooden stools there and we took our places in silence as outside the rain advanced with a hum, increasing in volume until it drowned out all other sounds. Everything had suddenly grown dark. The baby woke up and began to cry. The woman rocked it, then abruptly freed from her blouse a fat, round, flaccid breast that the infant greedily took hold of, suckling with all its strength. The rain was hammering the earth now and I watched the woman and her baby in silence, listening to the croaking of the toads that rose from the edge of the forest. Suddenly a shadow appeared in front of the shelter and shouted a few guttural words. The woman's face contorted, she hugged the child to her, the shadow had bent down to enter the shelter, when it straightened up I saw it was an armed soldier, his head covered in short braids and his chest and arms decorated with ill-assorted objects, jewelry or fetishes. He was shouting and waving us outdoors with his weapon, the woman had slipped from the chair and was seated on the ground, the baby still clutched in her arms, the man, without warning, started kicking me, I fell to the ground and he kept beating me until I began to crawl outside to escape him. The rain soaked me immediately, I tried to stand up, leaning on my hands, but a violent blow on my back sent me flying into a puddle. Dazed, groggy, my mouth full of mud that I spat out in vain, I curled up on my side, pain shooting through me like a burn from a red-hot iron, unable even to haul myself out of the puddle. Blurry, barely distinct, the green rubber boots of the man filled my entire field of vision, I rolled onto my shoulders as the green and brown figure, veiled by the rain, towered above me shaking his rifle, behind me the woman was screaming as well, I followed the soldier with my eyes as he joined her, she was convulsively clutching her baby, the man tore it away from her with a brutal gesture and sent it flying into a bush, the woman cried out and rushed toward the bush; but a violent rifle butt blow to her stomach made her double over, and she fell to the ground where the man kicked her in the head. I didn't see any more, something or rather someone had grabbed hold of my hair and was pulling me in the mud, I screamed and tried to grasp his arm, and got battered with blows for my trouble; I was suffocating, half smothered in mud and terror, finally I managed to rise to my knees as a relentless hand, twisting my arms behind my back, tied them together at the elbows. Then I was hauled to my feet and with a great shove propelled forward. It was almost night now, the rain blinded me and I could see nothing, a final blow threw me to the ground again near other people whom I could hear but not see. I twisted around to get back onto my knees, blinking frantically, I was surrounded by several heads, boys and girls, all looked very young and were shouting or crying in their language. The cord dug into my elbows and I could feel my hands growing numb. Little by little the rain grew lighter, a grey slice of sky appeared behind a cloud and shone a hesitant gleam on the scene. We were surrounded by soldiers, all looked like the first one, two of them were knotting ropes around the hips of the seated children, another came to tie me up in the same way, further on more soldiers, brandishing their automatic rifles, were pushing half a dozen men toward an immense solitary mango tree in the middle of the expanse of red earth, they stood them with their backs to the trunk and tied them together, the men let them without struggling, from where I was I couldn't hear if they were protesting or not, the rain was still falling a little and the croaking of toads filled the evening, the failing daylight drew gleams from the puddles scattered over the expanse, one of the soldiers picked up a big stick lying there and, with calm, precise, methodical gestures, smashed the heads of the men tied to the tree. Already other men were kicking us to make us stand up; I realized that we were all tied to each other to form a human chain, I seemed to be the only adult there, all the others looked like children or young adolescents. Two soldiers were standing near me: "Please, *s'il vous plait*, *bitte*, *por favor*, *min fadlikum*, *pozhaluysta*, *molim vas*," I mumbled idiotically in all the languages I knew, waving my arms behind my back. One of them glared at me with very red eyes; the other barked a few words, and the first took out a knife and came forward to cut the ropes digging into my elbows. My hands and forearms were blue, I no longer felt them at all, I struck them against my thighs and a horrible tingling filled them, almost unbearable, a burning pain also pulsed through my elbows where they had been tied and I massaged them as well as I could, clenching my teeth to avoid groaning. A little further away, a young girl was thrashing about on the ground and shouting. A soldier tried to stand her up but she resisted, striking the muddy ground with her feet and screaming with all her strength. Finally the soldier let her go and stood up, took the rifle from his shoulder, and crushed in her head with a few blows from the butt, stopping only when the girl had completely ceased twitching. Then he detached the rope from her hips and tied it again to reform the human chain that was already getting underway with shouts and blows, leaving the corpse stretched out in the mud, blood and splattered brain staining the puddles, still pricked by the last drops of rain.

They forced us to walk all night. Like all the children taken with me, I had to carry on my head a heavy bag full of grain or flour. The throbbing pain in my arms, injured by the overtight cords, made the exercise even more difficult; I kept slipping in the mud, tripping over roots, creepers, or brambles, often I dropped the bag and for my trouble received a volley of blows. Thorny branches scratched my arms and face, mosquitoes were devouring me and I couldn't even scratch the bites; I moved forward step by step, panting, roughly guided by the rope tying me to the young girl in front of me. Whenever one of the children, exhausted, wound up collapsing, they would shower him with kicks; if he didn't get up quickly enough, they would kill him, with a blow from a stick, the butt of a rifle, or a knife: ever since the appearance in the rain of the first soldier, I hadn't heard a single gunshot. Around us rose the immense trees of the forest, black and menacing, caught in a network of vegetation as in giant spiderwebs; the moonlight barely filtered through but that didn't seem to bother the soldiers leading the march. The darkness, on both sides of the column, was animated by the mad dance of fireflies, minuscule points of green light that appeared and disappeared, brief as a friendly wink; on all sides, the forest rustled, bird cries or monkeys frightened by the passing of the troop, sounds of crunching leaves, of broken branches, of drops of water shaken from branches, an order barked out in an unknown language, the yap of pain and fear of a child being hit, the hoarse noise of desperate breathing. Violent odors seized me in the throat, odors of earth, mud, swamp, decomposed leaves, the sharp smell of sweat from the soldiers who sometimes passed by me, the sweeter smell of shit when one of the children, unable to hold back anymore, shat while walking, the smell of fear, the most recognizable of all. When we arrived at the camp it was still night. Armed soldiers and a crowd of children welcomed us in a vast subdued murmur; bags, jerrycans, pots were taken off our heads by agile, almost invisible hands; separated into two groups, boys and girls, we were led, through a clearing still soaked with rain, before the leader of this strange army. Installed on a little seat made of woven wood, he sat in state beneath a straw awning, surrounded by a dozen soldiers armed with Russian rifles and machetes, young women and girls at his feet, sitting in silence. Rough hands forced us to our knees on the wet grass, a dozen meters from the group; the commander rose, the moon lit up his features and I could clearly make them out, he looked young, barely older than his men, I could see them better too and not one of them seemed to have passed adolescence. A soldier approached his chief, who, in a loud but slightly shrill voice, uttered several phrases, immediately translated by the soldier into a language that I understood no more than the original. Then the entire assembly knelt around us, the commander alone remaining standing, his little oiled braids and his gris-gris gleaming in the nighttime brightness, and intoned a solemn hymn, taken up in unison by all the others. When this was over, several soldiers passed among us, each holding a little gourd; at each new captive they dipped their fingers in the container and with a thick white substance drew a cross on his forehead, chest, back, and both hands. When my turn came, I submitted passively, closing my eyes; from now on, I belonged to them. Then the commander shared out the girls among his soldiers, keeping two for himself, and I was pushed with the other boys to a corner of the clearing, where we were again tied to each other by the waist and ordered to lie down and sleep. Above my head, the foliage of the trees stood out from the pale nighttime sky, a few drops were still falling from the leaves, the moon shone a little higher, and I could see no stars. A brief little cry sounded behind me, followed by a rustling of leaves and a grunt; I turned around as well as I could: in the midst of an expanse of tall green grass, near the first trees, a soldier had just pushed one of the girls onto the ground. She had fallen on her stomach, on the faintly golden ground, and he was lowering his pants and kneeling behind her to lift up her dress. She cried out again and he struck her, a brutal punch to the back of her neck; she fell abruptly silent, and he lay down on top of her; his black buttocks and his powerful thighs, almost blue in the cold light of the moon, were facing me, I watched them move in and out for a few moments, the girl's body had disappeared in the tall grass but I could sense her powerless trembling, finally I turned onto my back and closed my eyes. The respite didn't last long, a kick in the ribs woke me up too soon, all around me, in the dawn light, the camp was bustling about, young girls were pounding food in wooden mortars, boys were bringing in dead wood, fires were being made and water boiled. A few soldiers untied us and indicated that we could go into the woods to attend to our needs. I walked between the trees, distancing myself a little from the other boys and looking for a bush, and finally lowered my pants, stiff with mud and filth, and squatted: shit began to flow right away, liquid, stinking, almost green. When it was over I wiped myself as well as I could with some leaves and stood up. A little further on some soldiers were shouting, boys were running through the trees toward the camp. It was then that I noticed with surprise a hut, planted there on the edge of some land cleared between the trees, with earthen walls and a little wooden door. I approached and pulled the metal latch to push the door open, it gave way easily and I lowered my head and shoulders to enter. Once in the hallway I straightened up and despite the pain still shooting through my muscles immediately resumed running. I no longer felt either fatigue or discomfort, my breathing came easily and my long strides fell with regularity, even though I had trouble keeping my balance, I reeled a little, disoriented by the lack of light and landmarks, I bumped violently against a wall but didn't interrupt my running, gropingly searching for the way to navigate between the walls, avoiding the darker sections that could have turned out to be dungeons, or else side galleries leading God knows where. Finally I stumbled into the locker room and changed rapidly, pulling my swimming cap over hair still stiff with mud and going through the swinging doors to find myself in a large and very blue space echoing with shouts and water sounds. All around, long mirrors framing the pool sent back reflections of my body, fragmented and impossible to connect to each other, I tottered again, then pulled myself together, straightened up, and, body taut, buttocks tight, plunged straight as a spear into the clear, cool water.

II

I did lap after lap without counting them, reveling in the strength of my muscles and the fluid, viscous feel of the water, barely pausing at the ends of the pool before starting back again with a vigor each time renewed. Finally, plunged beneath the surface, eyes wide open, I finished. My head broke the surface, my hands found the edge, took hold, and, in one push of the shoulders, hauled my streaming body out of the water. Disoriented by the blue light and the sounds, I tore off my cap and goggles and stayed there for a moment, the water running from my body to form a puddle at my feet. The lapping of the water, shouts, laughter resounded around me, the large mirrors framing the pool reflected from every side fragments of my body, a shoulder here, a thigh there, the flank, the pectoral, the back of my neck, the curve of my back. Near me a slender girl dove into the water in a brief, powerful motion. I came to myself and headed for the swinging doors which I banged open with the palms of my hands. Dried off, wearing a silky grey tracksuit, pleasant to the skin, I found myself back in the hallway and began running in small strides, my white sneakers hitting the ground with a light step, my breathing whistling between my lips. A diffuse light reigned here, almost opaque, I could see no source of light and could just make out the walls enough to steer myself; in places, darker zones seemed to indicate intersections or perhaps some sort of gaps, I ignored them and continued straight on as well as I could as the hall seemed to curve and I constantly had to correct my course to avoid bumping into the walls. Sometimes, to guide myself, I held out my fingers, and this is how they collided with a metallic object, a handle which I grasped and pushed without hesitating, following the movement of the door that opened. I found myself in an unknown garden that nonetheless seemed vaguely familiar, an almost wild garden, abandoned, invaded by weeds. I made my way with difficulty between the long thorny branches of bougainvillea, half stifled by the ivy covering everything; in front of me, the tall façade of the house, raised like a tower, disappeared beneath the wisteria which proliferated up to the roof and twined together, or else fell back beneath its own weight, masking the sun and plunging the garden into a half-darkness that failed to mitigate the humid, heavy heat. I wiped off the sweat bathing my face with a sleeve and entered the house. Everything was quiet. Down the hallway, I pushed a half-open door: it was a child's room, I examined for a moment the toys, the movie posters, the tin cavalrymen scattered over the large carpet before turning back and climbing up the spiral staircase to the next floor. A framed reproduction of *Lady with an Ermine*, barely visible beneath the filth, decorated the landing; upstairs everything was empty. I passed my fingers over surfaces black with dust, thick, intact layers, as if the house had been abandoned long ago; nonetheless, I could discern everywhere traces of a recent presence, dirty dishes were piled in the sink, the fridge was full even though the food was beginning to stink, the irises in a narrow vase were only just wilting; in the dining room, the table was still set, the remnants of a meal filled the dishes and plates; clothes lay on the furniture, a book open on the sofa, an uncorked bottle on a cabinet. I climbed up to the next floor. The bedroom was dark, bathed in a weak greenish light, the daylight almost completely filtered by the wisteria covering the window. A suffocating heat reigned here and I tried to open the window, but the wisteria prevented me and I could only open it a crack. I wanted to turn on the lights but the bulbs seemed to have blown; I found a new one in a cupboard in the bathroom and changed the one in the bedside lamp, which still wouldn't light; I went back downstairs, found the fuse box in the kitchen, the fuses had blown and I reset the main circuit breaker, turning on several ceiling lamps in the process. Upstairs, the bedside lamp now threw a gloomy yellow light on the scene. I looked around me. At the foot of the bed lay piled a large embroidered bed-spread, long green grass on a golden background, negligently thrown there; women's clothes were scattered pretty much everywhere, dirty panties, skirts, mismatched shoes; on the dresser lay several photographs that I picked up and quickly examined, one after the other. They all showed me in the company of a beautiful little blond boy with lively, sparkling eyes, shown at different ages and in different situations, at the beach, at the circus, on a boat, but always near me, in my arms or sitting on my lap. I put them down and began searching through the drawers. In the nightstand, I found what I was looking for, a pair of scissors, made of very heavy metal; I picked up the photos again and began cutting them, separating my image from the little boy's, which I threw in the drawer that I closed when I was done. Then I shuffled the remaining pieces of the photos like a pack of cards and fanned them out. Abstracted thus from its context, my frozen face came to life, it reflected like a mirror the presence of the eliminated child, laying bare everything that connected it to him and that could never be undone. This aroused in me a glacial feeling, I couldn't tear my eyes away from these images and at the same time I couldn't look at them either; finally, overwhelmed with anguish, I threw them in a rage on the dresser where they fell, scattered.

In the kitchen, I searched through the fridge and the freezer in search of something edible; I finally found a few frozen langoustines that I sautéed in a saucepan with olive oil and garlic. I ate them with a delicious very cool white wine, separating the shell from the abdomens with my fingers and cracking the pincers between my teeth to suck out the fibers and juice. The meal over, I quickly cleared the dishes and carefully washed my fingers, which smelled of garlic and seafood, before returning to finish the wine with a thin little cigar in front of the bay window in the living room, contemplating the saffron light of evening through the tangle of wisteria. When the light faded completely I lit the living room lamps, one by one. I also tried to put a disk on, but the stereo was dead, something must have blown. Finally, I went upstairs. Near the bed, the bedside lamp still illumined the bedroom with its dirty light; my gaze ran over the wrinkled, unclean, stained sheets; when I tried to beat the pillow, a cloud of dust rose up, making me sneeze several times. Annoyed, I took off the pillowcase and removed the sheets, then dug into a cupboard to find clean ones and hastily remade the bed. I dragged the bedspread to the stairway to shake it; the space filled with dust, I slapped it several times against the stone steps, sneezing convulsively, before returning to throw it over the sheets. Through the gaps in the wisteria, the moonlight barely filtered, spotting with little white dots the long green grass and the golden background of the cloth. I quickly got undressed; a fine layer of sweat covered my skin, it was still just as hot, I felt as if I were suffocating. I lay down on my belly, stretching out my arms and stroking with my fingers the thick weft of the embroidery. My member had gotten stuck under my stomach and I freed it; my buttocks prickled and I turned around to look at the tall upright mirror standing near the door: but it reflected nothing other than an empty corner of the bed, a section of white wall, the edge of the window. I fell asleep this way, my naked body on the grass of the bedspread, bathed in that uneven, hesitant light. An indefinable noise drew me from a dream where I was trying to convince a young blond woman, her bun artfully disheveled, to take driving lessons. Without turning around, I looked over my shoulder toward the door: it was open now, whereas I was sure I had closed it. The black rectangle of the stairway stood out from the doorframe, I scrutinized this darkness, in vain, there was nothing there. When I woke again the sky, behind the wisteria, seemed to be growing pale. Apart from a very slight rustling of leaves there was still no sound. I got up, quickly pulled on my tracksuit and went down to the living room. In front of the kitchen door, I briefly entertained the idea of making myself coffee, but I immediately gave it up and went down to the lower floor. In the child's room, I tried to head toward the bed, but the tin cavalrymen scattered over the carpet were in my way, I was afraid of crushing them and I remained for a moment near the door, contemplating the empty bed and the sheets rolled in a ball, before turning round and walking down the hall to emerge into the garden. Dead leaves and twigs crackled beneath my feet, the morning heat clung to my skin, the profusion of uncontrolled vegetation filled me with a dull, vague anxiety. I headed for the door at the back which opened easily beneath the pressure of my hand. As soon as it closed behind me I began to run, relieved by the relative coolness that reigned here. The cadence of my breathing gave rhythm to my stride; everything seemed slightly blurred, indistinct, I couldn't even see the ceiling, if there was one, but that didn't bother me, I could guess at, more than I could make out with precision, the walls, the darker grey that here and there indicated a juncture or at least a recessed corner, I avoided all obstacles to follow the long sinuosity of the corridor, cheerfully striking a wall from time to time to assure myself of its solidity and of the softness of its covering. This is how my hand fell on a metal protuberance: I grasped it, turned, and pushed. Past the threshold my foot burrowed into something soft and I stopped short. I found myself in a rather large room, quite clear, sparsely furnished; on the walls, the

golden vines of the wallpaper intertwined up to the mold-
ings; a dark red, almost blood-colored carpet covered the
floor. Across the room, separated from me by a bed covered
in a heavy golden cloth embroidered with long green grass,
stood a figure with close-cropped jet black hair. The shutters
were closed, but it was staring at something in the window,
perhaps its own reflection. I gently pushed the door, which
closed with a muffled sound; the figure turned round, and I
saw then that it was a man, a handsome young man who as
he saw me let a fleeting little smile cross his dark, angular
face. He was of an unreal, almost perfect beauty, a beauty
that definitively isolated him from the world. With a supple,
feline motion, he skirted round the bed and without a word
grasped my neck to draw my mouth against his. His stubble
scratched my skin, but I greedily returned his kiss, at once
intoxicated and put off by his smell of cheap cologne mixed
with musky sweat. In one motion, he laid me down on the
green leaves of the bedspread and knelt above me, leaning on
his powerful arms, which I stroked with my fingertips along
with his shoulders, neck, and sides. My member, stuck a little
sideways, hardened beneath the tracksuit; he straightened
up, I held out my hands and began undoing the buckle of
his heavy leather belt, he withdrew some more and stood
up, my fingers searched to free his member, wedged beneath
the elastic of the briefs, finally it came free, swollen already,
soft and firm, and I leaned over to lick its tip before sliding it between my lips, it hardened some more and filled
my mouth, pressing against my tongue and the back of my
throat, I rolled it between my lips, savoring its sweetness
and its power, his hand, on the nape of my neck, pushed

me against the curls of his pubis, I breathed through my nose, driven to a frenzy by his insipid, acrid smell of urine and deodorant, sucking in the taut member with my tongue and lips, finally a retch made me gag and I tore myself away from him, swallowing convulsively. His moist cock struck my cheek as he emitted a brief chuckle, his hand still pressed against the back of my neck. I wanted to bring my mouth to his member again but he took a few steps back, letting it beat to the rhythm of his heart between the open fly of his jeans before shoving it back into his briefs and buttoning everything up. "Wait. I'm hungry." He picked up the receiver next to the bed, dialed a number and, holding up a cardboard menu, named a few items. I rose, shaking my numb legs, and went into the bathroom, where I opened wide the heavy porcelain faucets of the shower, one hand under the stream of water to gauge the temperature.

Under the scalding water he rubbed against me, gripping my ass and pressing me against him, his still half erect member knocking against my own. I turned him around to soap his shoulders, his back, his hips, gliding my fingers between his buttocks and caressing the tufts of curly hairs around his anus. His matte skin was covered with numerous little scars, thick enough in places to form bumps, I counted three on his shoulder and could feel a few more beneath my fingers, on his chest and his groin, and also a long forked one at the angle of his jaw. I pressed my sex against his ass and bit the nape of his neck as he leaned against the tiled wall. Muffled knocks sounded on the bedroom door. He broke away, running his fingers along my balls and member, and slipped on a large terrycloth robe before going to the door. I relaxed in the stream of water, bending my neck under the scalding pressure. A powerful desire filled me, stretching my muscles with excitation while leaving me racked with an empty, sated feeling. Finally I turned off the water and dried off quickly, putting on the other bathrobe hanging there without taking the trouble of closing it. Sitting cross-legged on the green and gold bedspread, the young man was contemplating a large tray on which were lined up dishes in lacquered wood, filled with raw fish and pickled vegetables. Two golden beers frothed in tall, slightly tapered glasses. I joined him and began eating in silence. Aside from the clicking of the chopsticks there was no sound; behind the shutters, which, I supposed, looked out on a street or a courtyard, everything was quiet; a lone lamp, by the bedside, lit us with its pale halo, and I could clearly see our reflections in the windowpanes, two slightly blurred silhouettes, draped in white, which stood out from the verdant field of the bedspread. I finished the last little vegetables, pushed away the tray, and began undoing the knot of his bathrobe, sliding my hand between his thighs to stroke his member. He let out a long sigh and fell back on the bedspread. I spread his legs and leaned forward to run my tongue around his balls and then roll them between my lips, one after the other. With both hands, I pushed his knees back, almost to his shoulders, and continued licking him, sliding my tongue along the perineum and burrowing between the hairs, flicking the tip, to finally come and tickle his anus. It had a slightly spicy, sour taste, I buried my tongue in as he sighed and stroked my hair with one hand, pulling his calves even further back. It was very dry in that room, I quickly lacked saliva; I let his legs go and straightened up to drink a little beer, he took the glass from my hands and drank too, then in a swift motion he shed his bathrobe and turned over onto his belly, offering me his downy thighs and powerful, muscular buttocks; I stripped in turn and stretched on top of him, my stiff member pressed between his thighs, I took his chin in my hand and turned his head toward mine, his lips still had the bitter taste of the beer, I lifted his pelvis and with one hand guided my member toward the opening of his anus, but it was too dry, so I straightened up and brought some saliva up on my tongue as with both hands I spread his buttocks, the saliva streamed onto his hairs and his puckered, barely dilated anus, I massaged it with my thumb, which I dug in a little, and also coated my member with saliva. Then I pressed it again in the center of the hairs, he grunted, pushed as well, it opened all of a sudden and I found myself sucked in, glued against his ass, I slid my hands under his armpits and closed them over the back of his neck, gripping onto him and forcing into him with large thrusts, he moaned, his face pressed in the green leaves of the bedspread, I lifted his pelvis some more and turned around: in the panes of the window, I could clearly make out our two bodies on top of each other, the twin moon of my ass and my spread thighs, suspended above his with between them a darker, indistinct mass. Already pleasure was bursting open my back, stretching the skin of my neck; I slowed down; just at that moment, the phone rang, freezing us on top of each other. As I withdrew to pick it up, I squeezed the muscles of my pelvis with all my strength, but it was too late, pleasure had overcome me and my sperm, as I articulated a hoarse

"Yes?" into the receiver, spurted out in long jerks, spattering my stomach, the boy's ass, the embroidered leaves of the bedspread. "Yes?" In the receiver, no one replied. I pressed my ear to it, repeated several times "Hello? Hello?" but I could hear only the light buzzing of the empty line. Still lying on his stomach, the young man was quickly jerking off, I finally hung up and grasped his ass and balls with both hands, clenching my fingers as he came in turn.

An electrical outage plunged us into darkness as I tried to wipe the traces of sperm from the bedspread with the help of a roll of toilet paper. I lay down next to the boy, who turned his back to me with a sigh that was hard to interpret. I pressed against him, my now-soft member nestled in the hollow of his buttocks. We must have fallen asleep that way. The return of electricity woke me suddenly. My mouth was dry, pasty; blinking, I dragged myself out of bed to go drink greedily from the bathroom faucet, briefly blinded by the neon light that I turned off right away. Emerging from the bathroom I contemplated the boy: he was still sleeping, sprawled out on his belly, his downy legs intertwined with the embroidered cloth. I slowly ran the pads of my fingers along his back and buttocks, tripping over the scars; his skin grated, almost rough; between his legs, my sperm had dried in long whitish trails. I should turn down the heat, I thought confusedly. But I could see no thermostat, no temperature control. Finally I filled two glasses with water and put them on the radiator before turning off the light and lying back down alongside the young man, one hand on his side. Sounds of water emanating from the bathroom woke me completely.

The light was on again and I was alone on the bed. I knocked on the bathroom door and went in without waiting for a reply: the young man, standing in front of the toilet, was peeing. I kissed his shoulder and quickly rinsed off in the shower. When I emerged, a towel knotted around my waist, he had just finished putting on his jeans and buckling his belt. With a smile I tapped the bulge formed by his limb: "Nice package," I said. He chuckled dryly, slipped his t-shirt over his head, pulled a cellphone from his pocket and consulted it: "I have to go. Will you give me the money?" I looked at him with surprise: "The money?"—"Yes, the money. Like always." He was sitting on the edge of the bed now and was pulling on his socks and leather ankle boots. A dull anxiety was seeping into my muscles; I hesitated, then went to search through the pockets of my tracksuit before returning with a helpless gesture. The boy had gotten up and was standing in front of me, his shoulders hunched a little and his face calm and cold; a threatening feeling emanated from him, not from his face but from his rounded shoulders, the tension of his thighs, the deceptive calmness of his dangling arms. "Well?"—"I don't have any money, actually."—"Are you fucking with me, or what?" His arm straightened and before I could make a move of defense he slapped me across the face, sending me into the wall; another blow, with his closed fist to my belly, doubled me over and sent me to my knees in front of him, stunned, my breath cut off. He took me by the hair, straightened me up, and struck me again several times in the face, sending me flying onto the bed where my mouth splattered the heavy cloth of the bedspread with blood. "Are you fucking with me?" He chased me through the room, the towel had fallen and I crawled naked as he rained my ribs and limbs with kicks, which exploded in my body like bursts of fire. Finally he left me sprawled on the carpet, my mouth and nose full of blood, wheezing and struggling to breathe in a little air. The backs of his legs were in front of me, I saw my clothes fall to the floor one after the other. "Fuck, you really don't have anything, you son of a bitch," his voice said far above my head as his legs turned toward me. I saw the tip of one of his boots draw back, then nothing. When I came to I was still lying thus, naked on the carpet soaked in blood; fortunately, the color was the same, it wasn't too visible. I stayed there for a while panting, letting the pain shoot through my body, then I dragged myself to the bathroom where I managed to haul myself up to the sink. I rinsed off my face, my mouth; the water, turned red, splattered the sink and mirror, I delicately felt my nose and my teeth, one or two moved a little but they were all there, my nose didn't seem broken, I kept drinking and rinsing off until the water ran almost clear. Then I returned to the bedroom where I gathered my clothes with difficulty and sat down like a block on the edge of the bed to put them on, painfully. Finally dressed, I leaned back for a few minutes to catch my breath, then headed for the door. There were in fact two, I hadn't noticed, and I had no idea which one had been taken by the young man, whom I had no wish to cross paths with again. I opened one at random and went out. Immediately the cool air of the hallway invigorated me, the pain racking my limbs faded away and I began running in short strides, setting one foot regularly in front of the other and breathing with ease. It wasn't so dry anymore and quickly a fine layer of sweat covered my face and my bruised body; swallowing saliva, I could still taste the sharp, slightly ferruginous hint of blood; I pressed my tongue against my teeth, it hurt but they held firm. Everything was very grey here, my sight remained blurry and I could make out almost nothing, barely, perhaps, a few slightly darker rectangles which could just as easily have been nooks or alcoves as junctions, I tried to remain in the center of the hallway, which wasn't easy since it kept curving, from time to time I almost collided with a wall and I would stumble as I recovered, but never did I stop running, I set one foot in front of the other while holding out a hand, fingers open, to assure myself of where the walls were, and that's how I noticed somewhat by chance a metallic object, a doorknob apparently, my fingers closed on it and pushed and the door opened all of a sudden. I followed it and without letting go crossed the threshold. The space that opened up before me, a vast studio, welcomed me like a refuge and I crossed it, staggering, leaning on the walls and the bookcases that covered them, to reach the large bay window in the back, in front of which I collapsed into a black leather armchair. I felt disoriented, empty of thought but terribly ill at ease with myself, it wasn't the physical pain which had already almost disappeared, no, it was something else, a numb anxiety that bored into my mind and kept me from enjoying the peaceful view in front of me, piles of colorful little buildings, rising in levels in front of the double wall formed by the long blue strip of the sea and the paler strip, veering to grey at the edge of the horizon, of the sky. I stayed there for a long time, breathing through my lips, before hauling myself painfully out of the armchair to stroll through the studio. A disk case was lying on the stereo, old recordings of Mozart piano concertos, but I had no desire for music and I left it there. Everything seemed futile to me, emptied of meaning and interest, the books lined up on the shelves, the reproductions and engravings hanging on the walls. I poured myself a glass of schnapps, drank it down, and poured another before burrowing into the sofa, black leather like the armchair, rolling between my fingers a little cigar, which I didn't light. An album was lying there on the coffee table, I leafed through it absentmindedly: in oblong format, bound in white cloth, it showed naked women and men, executing various movements broken down into stop motion sequences by a multiple camera setup. I didn't pause at any plate in particular, they passed in front of my eyes, a frozen series of backs, thighs, and white asses, seized for eternity by the successive triggering of the shutter in poses that no longer formed a single movement but served rather to emphasize these white bodies and what they were reduced to, backs, asses, and thighs.

It was cool in this apartment, almost cold. I searched through the cupboards for something to eat and threw together a scant meal of sardines in oil, raw onion, black bread, and rosé. I finished the bottle, my body already trembling with cold under my thin tracksuit; I had barely finished clearing away when I felt my abdomen contract, the meal came back up suddenly, the still cold wine mixed with the remnants of onions and sardines in a thick mush that splattered the sink; it eased up a little and I ran with my hand in front of my mouth to the bathroom, everything came up again and I finished emptying myself out in the white porcelain toilet bowl, tears in my eyes, my throat burned by the acid mixture, my stomach twisted by spasms. When it was over I rinsed my mouth out thoroughly, then sat on the floor to catch my breath. Finally I got up. In the kitchenette, I poured myself a large glassful of schnapps and drained it in one swallow, it added to the burning sensation but slightly masked the foul taste that still filled my mouth. I washed the sink as well as I could and returned to the bathroom to run a shower, waiting for the water to get hot before undressing and plunging in. The water struck my exhausted body without reinvigorating it, I found it hard to get my bearings, I ran my hands along my sides, my hips, my ass, and my thighs without managing to find the sense of this body that was crumbling and escaping me. In the bedroom, I dried myself off in front of a large round mirror leaning at the foot of the bed, a simple mattress placed on the floor and covered with an embroidered bedspread, quite thick, of long green grass on a golden background. My body in the mirror seemed inscrutable to me, I abstractly contemplated the limbs and torso marbled with blue and black spots veering to green, only the veined member, forgotten and useless between the thighs, seemed to distinguish it from a woman's body, it was in any case a vague, indistinct body, and when I turned around it became even more so, reduced to a few illuminated lines, curves and sections of skin that could have belonged to anyone. I knelt down on the bedspread, back to the mirror; turning my head I could see the white globes of the buttocks and nestled between them the brown recess of the anus, I squeezed my thighs to hide the balls, thus leaving in my field of vision only the behind, the anus and the green grass of the bedspread, I pulled on the buttocks and the anus dilated a little, opening up like an iris onto its unfathomable depth, a black hole that seemed the only part still whole of this body slowly breaking up, struggling in the mirror to reorganize itself around it. I wet a finger with saliva and ran it over the edge of the cavity, pressing in little circles, then closed my eyes and inserted one fingertip, the contact reassured me and I pushed some more, it spread a sensation of well-being all around that diffused itself throughout my frozen body, outlining a shape for it, still approximate, but quite real. The intercom buzzed and I withdrew the finger, opening my eyes. I waited. It buzzed again, in long repeated rings, grating. I got up and with the same finger I had just withdrawn from my body angrily pressed on the button: "Yes?" I barked. A woman's voice replied, a gentle and firm voice, the voice of a blond woman I thought without understanding how I could know that. "Sir," she said, "I also live in this building, and your electric circuit is having strong surges that are causing outages for all your neighbors. This has to stop." Anger swelled my face and I shouted into the intercom with a broken, trembling voice: "Madam, I've had that circuit completely overhauled by a professional electrician, twice in a row. That's enough, now!" I yanked my finger from the button, then switched off the intercom so it couldn't ring again. Still furious, at a loss, I lay down on the bedspread, on my belly with my arms spread out, and abruptly fell asleep. When I woke up I was trembling with cold. I got up and wrapped the bedspread around my shoulders, then crossed the studio in the darkness to go stand in front of the bay window. Below, I could see in the darkness a lozenge of light, the window of a neighboring apartment forming a section crossed lengthwise by a long sofa upholstered in white upon which had sunk a naked young woman, quickly followed by a man with an erection. He lifted her legs to enter her, moving in and out with a regular, jerky, almost mechanical rhythm, then turned her over on her knees and resumed his motion, still to the same rhythm. After a few minutes they changed positions once again, this time he was seated on the sofa and she was crouching over him, but the rhythm remained the same, almost comical, the rhythm of an old Buster Keaton film shot at sixteen frames per second, they tried out one after another in this way as if they were systematically attempting all the positions recommended by some German sex manual for couples, I watched a while more the doubled moons of their asses, facing the luminous lozenge of the window, then wearied of that and returned to lie down on the mattress, still rolled in the bedspread that protected me a little from the coolness of the night. I dreamed of endless, poorly executed construction work, and also of a blond woman, my mother or my wife, I couldn't be sure, who didn't know how to drive and didn't want to learn. When I woke up again a cold light fell in the room, making the golden fabric of the cloth sparkle but warming nothing. I got up and dressed quickly, swallowed a glass of juice, and headed for the door. As I opened it I hesitated, hand on the knob, something was vaguely holding me back, the voice of the woman in the intercom perhaps, but this fleeting feeling faded as quickly as it had appeared, I pulled the door open and went out. Immediately a soft warmness invaded my limbs, and, suddenly relaxed, I began running with a regular, none-too-rapid pace, elbows in at my body, breathing with ease and focusing on the floor in front of my feet, as grey and hard to place with precision as the walls or the ceiling, quasi-invisible in the darkness, if there even was one, who knows, perhaps this long hallway was open to the outside, one couldn't be sure of anything. From time to time, one of my sleeves grazed a wall; then I would instinctively correct my course, trying to follow the imperceptible curve without deviating, paying no attention to the darker zones that could just as easily have turned out to be recesses as security shelters or else other hallways, leading God knows where. I felt no difficulty in this running, I breathed with ease, filling my lungs and supplying my body with oxygen as it went forward in a supple, regular, even stride. A brilliant little spot, on one of the walls, drew my attention, it was a door handle and I opened it, passing the threshold without slowing down. Two steps further I had to pull up short to avoid bumping into a naked man who favored me with a reptilian look, at once puzzled and empty, before stepping back and then moving away. Another man, his arms and thighs covered with abstract motifs tattooed in black ink, had just finished undressing; still another was pulling on his member and his balls to slip a sort of metal ring over them. The air was damp, gorged with humidity, but it was cooler here than in the hallway, I was still sweating and began to undress in turn, opening one of the many white lockers that covered the walls to throw my clothes in. A young man handed me a bath towel, some flip-flops, and a padlock; I sealed the locker and tied the towel around my waist, then followed the other men who had disappeared in the darkness in back of the little room. The floor, tiled and wet, was a little slippery, an indefinable, irritating smell filled the air; I emerged at a little bar around which stood a few men, in towels or completely naked aside from their flip-flops. A smiling, well-built young man, his muscles thin but defined, both nipples pierced with little rings, came up to me and put his hand on my shoulder: "What will you have?"— "Whatever you like." While the bartender was mixing the cocktails the young man stared at me mistrustfully; as I tasted my gin and tonic, clear, cool, sparkling, almost bitter, he leaned over and breathed a few words in my ear: "Do you come here often?"—"I don't know. It depends."—"I don't remember seeing you. But it's true that you don't come to look." He moved away to join his companions, leaving me to drink alone. I quickly finished the glass and headed for the staircase, which led to the lower floor. The smell intensified as I descended, growing more precise, it stank of rancid male sweat and dirty socks, mixed with strong animal effluvia, hints of sperm and of shit. Below, a dark labyrinth of hallways, cubicles and recesses opened up on several sides, guarded by a large black man, naked and motionless. I briefly contemplated his impassive face, his muscular chest, his thick, long member, then headed for the showers where I rinsed off my body before going to sit down in a very hot cubicle, full of steam. Other men were sharing it with me, no one spoke, I didn't stay long and went out to shower again before returning, flip-flops slapping on the flagstones, toward the black Cerberus who didn't seem to have moved an inch. Having come up even with him, I hesitated, then brushed my fingers over his hip bone; he pulled away, his gaze still distant, I didn't insist and entered the labyrinth, moving slowly in the half-darkness. Men stood here and there, most of them in towels, barely discernible silhouettes in the darkness, some standing in the hallway, others sitting in a cubicle, hands on their members or behind their necks. As I passed them I could hear an almost imperceptible murmur, words perhaps but impossible to understand, or maybe also just inarticulate sounds, groans interspersed with stammering cries. In one room, very vaguely lit, several naked men, gleaming with sweat, were busying themselves around another man, suspended with his legs in the air in a sort of leather hammock; further on, in a little, almost completely dark cubicle, a man with hairy shoulders and a powerful back, crouching over another man's thighs, was moving his hips in and out, without a sound. At random, I tried to approach one of the men stationed in the hallway, placing my hand on his chest, but he pushed it away without a word and I went on my way, repeating the operation with every man I passed, with as little success. Vexed, I ventured into a cubicle where a naked man, completely hairless, rather plump, was lying on a banquette, his towel over his face; I approached, he didn't react, I placed my hand on his limp member: this contact provoked no movement, not even a start. I took his parts in my fingers and stroked them slowly, the man still didn't budge, so I leaned over and slipped the member between my lips, it remained limp, I rolled it in my mouth while squeezing the balls a little, then I began sucking it, suckling as if it were an udder, but there was nothing to be done, it didn't harden, finally I straightened up and left the man sprawled there to resume my movements through the hallway. In the back, I discovered a little round room with a basin full of bubbling water: the young man who had offered me a drink was immersed in it up to his chest in the company of two other men, inhaling, with a glass straw, some white powder arranged in rows on a little tray. When he saw me he handed me the tray and the straw, without a word I grasped it delicately and imitated him, inhaling first one line, then another; a shiver ran through my body, I passed the tray to his neighbor and straightened up, balanced tensely on my thighs, smoothing the towel with one hand over my hip and buttocks. I would have liked to slip into the water with them but there was no more room; so I turned around and once again penetrated the labyrinth. Here and there men were sucking a member, licking an ass, or penetrating each other, there weren't many single men and these, inexplicably, scorned my advances, they seemed to prefer to remain solitary, standing stiff in the dark, their eyes empty, slowly stroking themselves. In the room with the hammock, the suspended young man was alone now, sprawled with his head back, his legs dangling, his body stained with sperm and marbled with traces of blows or cigarette burns, emptied, inert, lost in another space. I could have lifted his legs and screwed him myself, but I preferred to remain there and watch him softly moan, withdrawn into himself and very far away, I envied him and would have certainly liked to be in his place, but it appeared I hadn't mastered the obscure rules of this place, for no one wanted me. I lay down for a long while in a cubicle, my ass facing the entrance, the cocaine buzzing through my body, but no one came to caress me or take what I was so willingly offering; from time to time, I sensed a vague presence in the opening but when I turned around it had already disappeared; exasperated, I finally got up, elsewhere it was the same thing, the black giant, at the entrance, when I squatted down in front of him to take his heavy, veined member in my mouth, gave me a clout that sent me flying onto my ass, in the room in the back they gave me more cocaine without batting an eyelid but no one made room for me in the basin, the excitement spread through my body gave me no respite and sent me for yet another expedition into the labyrinth, just as vain, finally I returned to the sauna, letting the moist heat relax somewhat my enervated body, tensed to the breaking point.

Afterward, I went under the shower again; the cold water beat against my face, which I pictured prematurely aged, worn out, wearied by desire. When I emerged I saw, beyond the sauna and the labyrinth, a room that I hadn't noticed before: behind a large glass wall, standing in the half-light, half a dozen naked men were intertwined. I watched them for a while, then joined them, and this time no one tried to push me away. I was very quickly pulled in by the press of bodies, hands ran over my body and massaged my buttocks, moist fingers came to knead my anus, stubbly faces pressed their lips against mine, mouths sucked then painfully bit my nipples, my own hands, gropingly, found stiff members and stroked them, the smell of rancid sweat and flesh intoxicated me and I was losing my bearings, I found myself on my knees, a cock pressed into the back of my throat, another rubbing against my cheek, a third beating against my forehead, powerful, dominating grips held my hair and neck and directed my head, members knocked against my rounded lips and pressed against my palate, half suffocating me, they finally withdrew and a pair of hairy buttocks took their place, pressed against my face, I stuck out my tongue and absorbed the acrid, bitter taste of the anus, another tongue, greedily, was doing the same with mine, boring into it as several hands spread my buttocks, little by little I found myself pressed to the ground, an arm or a foot wedged my neck there and my ass was pulled up for a first member to come plant into it, I grunted under the pressure of the arm and was rewarded by having my head lifted up for another cock to bury in my mouth, both members moved in and out inside me, quartering me and filling me with a white fire that shot right through me, making me tremble with pleasure so strongly that hands had to support me so I wouldn't collapse, the man behind me was forcing my ass held almost vertically with large thudding strokes, finally he stiffened completely, overcome by pleasure, his cock quivered as it emptied itself and then, before it had even gone limp, withdrew all of a sudden, dragging behind it the flaccid latex of the condom full of sperm, another immediately took its place and everything started over again, in my mouth as well one member followed another, I had lost all notion of time, a man came abruptly on my face and the sperm, sticky, covered my eyes and lips, I wiped it off as well as I could and blinked to unstick the eyelids, I was surrounded by fragments of bodies, hands, thighs, hairy or else clean-shaven and tattooed, thick cocks, erect with their foreskins pulled back, I closed my eyes and gave in to all these members that kneaded me, pierced me, opened me even wider, my body seemed impossibly rounded, enlarged like a corolla swollen with sap, arched also by the discharges of pleasure that tensed it to the breaking point before suddenly letting it go, instantly resuming their increasing pulsations, it overwhelmed my senses and exhausted my muscles that trembled more than ever, I opened my eyes, the glass wall, near me, vaguely reflected the intermingling of bodies, I could make out nothing with precision except asses, superimposed and shining like moons, behind the window too there was a figure, I opened my eyes wide to discern it better, it was a little child, a blond boy with a pointy face, completely naked, who was watching us through the glass wall with his eyes wide open, his lips stubborn, obstinate. I froze, the face too remained immobile, around me the throng of bodies staggered, grunted, panted; a diffuse uneasiness filled me, quickly detaching me from my own body. What was this boy doing here? I wondered. Wasn't admittance to this establishment forbidden to minors? The boy, silent and willful, kept staring at me, and I tried to free myself from the man who was brutally penetrating me, but his hands gripped my hips and held me pitilessly riveted to his member which went in and out at a frantic pace, I pushed him away in vain, the little boy never took his eyes off us, panic submerged me and I struggled even more, other hands came to twist my arms and pin my shoulders again to the ground, a foot crushed my head against the tiles as the limb withdrew all of a sudden to splatter my ass with cum, already another was taking its place to come delight in me, then I closed my eyes, instantly erasing both the little boy and the organs surrounding me, and I surrendered to the storm of flesh, my body as if torn away from itself, splashing everything around it before being carried away by a black, raging sea.

When I opened my eyes again I was alone, lying on the tiled floor. I turned onto my back and instinctively covered my parts with my hands, as if to protect them from blows that didn't come. Streaks of sperm were drying on my skin, smearing my face, my hair. I thought of the young man in the hammock, abandoned to himself; I too, now, must have looked just as overcome. But my mind couldn't manage to detach itself from my body, bruised, racked, weighted down. I hadn't come yet and I feebly tried to jerk off, but my member refused to harden and I finally got up and went to shower. I remained for a long while under the stream of water, my legs still trembling, my limbs shattered with fatigue, I let my head and neck roll under the stream which little by little rinsed off all the filth stuck to my skin and warmed my muscles. Finally I turned off the water and headed for the stairway. My towel had disappeared and I was walking naked, still dripping. On my way, I passed several men, they didn't pay the slightest attention to me and there was no way of knowing if they had been part of those who had used me or not. I felt only a vague curiosity about it, almost abstract, amused even. At the bar, I asked for a towel, dried myself and wrapped it around my hips, then ordered a gin and tonic which I went to sip on a mock leather sofa, facing a television screen where pornographic scenes were playing with the sound turned off. The images, changing but repetitive, flashed before my gaze, which, at times, absentmindedly focused on them, but immediately it would shift away, nothing caught it, it had become as indifferent to the series of swollen cocks penetrating series of round, white asses as to the large photographs of expanses of tall grass, shining on a golden ground, which covered the wall behind the bar. Aside from the bar-tender, there was almost no one left, near me a man was drinking a soda and tugging in boredom on his sex while staring at the screen with a glum, empty gaze, I finished my cocktail, got up, and returned to the locker room. My body was still vibrating, overtaxed by sensations but always avid, I vaguely hoped to meet the young man with the pierced nipples, the one who had bought me a drink when I arrived, I wanted to offer him one in turn and then greedily caress his sleek, beautiful body, but there was no one and I took my clothes out of the locker, put them on, and headed for the door. It opened easily and as soon as I passed through it I began running again. The effort invigorated my exacerbated muscles, I felt them relax and rediscover their natural, orderly sense of balance which propelled me with an even stride, neither too slow nor too fast, timed to the breathing that whistled between my lips. In the half-darkness that reigned here, I guessed at more than saw the walls of the hallway, they seemed to be curving and I regularly had to adjust my course so as not to collide with one, at times darker parts seemed to indicate a junction or even a kind of crypt, I ignored them and ran with my head empty, not thinking of anything, happy with the easy deployment of my body, which adjusted quite naturally to the unfolding of this space whose end could not be guessed, I felt like a child free of all constraint and didn't worry about anything, here and there my fingers gaily beat against the walls, for fun as much as to ensure my orientation, and this is how they encountered a kind of metal projection, a door handle it seemed, on which I leaned and pushed, opening a door through which I passed without slowing down, in a supple bound. My sneakers crunched in the snow and I stopped. A man passed in front of me, leading a horse by a tether, followed by two men carrying a cooking pot, their frozen breath hung suspended in the frigid air that cut through the thin cloth of my tracksuit. I shivered and rubbed my arms. A little further on, under a large beech tree with bare, grey branches, a group of men were crowded around a fire. I approached, my feet sinking into the fresh snow; one of the men noticed me and called out to me: "Well now, sir! You'll catch cold like that. Come change." He led me toward a little hut where I found in a rough wardrobe made of boards everything I needed: pants of solid brown material and a turtleneck sweater, which I pulled on over my tracksuit, an officer's jacket with golden buttons, leather boots, and a long, thick, high-collared coat, with heavy folds that beat against my calves. There was also a fur hat and a close-fitting pair of white gloves, which I put on and buttoned with a remarkable feeling of satisfaction. The soldier was waiting for me at the door: "Don't forget this," he said, handing me a riding crop and a leather holster that contained a heavy long-barreled pistol with a rounded butt made of polished wood. Snow was starting to fall, a drift of flakes light as air that danced gaily and melted at the slightest contact. I fastened the holster to the belt of my jacket as I followed the soldier to the fire. Other men had come join the first group, they all wore a uniform similar to mine; when they saw me approach they stood to attention, clicked their heels, and saluted me. Several of them were wearing a heavy, wrought metal cross around their neck; I took my own out of my jacket pocket and placed it around my neck too, softly caressing the metal with my fingers before lifting my head up toward a naked man, hanged by a single foot to a branch of the beech, his grey skin lacerated with blows and gashes. "This one?"—"A spy, sir. He was prowling around the horses, we gave him a good lesson." I nodded and approached the blaze. A man slid over a folding stool on which I sat, another handed me a tin spoon and a steaming bowl filled with red beans. I was very hungry and I cheerfully devoured the dish, it lacked salt but that didn't matter, I swallowed the last spoonful and scraped the bowl. I was now completely warmed up, the fire was pleasantly roasting my feet and thighs, a few snowflakes stuck for an instant to my sleeves before melting and I contemplated them with pleasure. I belched and drank some water. "Have the horses saddled," I ordered as I got up. "We're leaving." Immediately, the men began to bustle about. Above the fire, the hanged man swayed gently, held in place by a thinner branch impaled in his anus. A soldier came up to me and saluted: "What about the prisoners, sir?" I thought about it for an instant: "Shoot them."—"The women too?"—"The women too." I headed in long strides for the enclosure. A man was leading toward me a handsome bay horse, whose nostrils exhaled spirals of steam that mixed with snowflakes, falling thicker and thicker. I took the tether from the soldier's hands, patted the animal's neck, checked the girth, and hauled myself onto the saddle, where I settled to watch the preparations. In my jacket pocket I found a cigar case; I lit one and drew on it, immediately the puffs of tobacco brought me a sensation of serenity, light and almost joyful like the snow filling the sky. Around me, men were coming and going, lining up the horses, striking the tents; further on, some soldiers were escorting a small group of men and women, most of them dressed in rags. Having reached a copse of pine trees, they forced them to kneel in the snow. Then a soldier pointed his rifle, aimed at a neck, and pressed the trigger; the man flew forward in a sudden spurt of blood; already the soldier was moving on to the next one and adjusting his weapon. Men on horseback came and joined me. One of them handed me a spear, with the handle made of polished ash and a long, sharp, thin blade shaped like a leaf; I grasped it joyfully, hefting it and then placing it across my knees. When everything was ready I took a last puff on the cigar, threw the butt into the snow and brandished the spear to give the signal for departure. My horse pawed the ground and I guided it with my heels, slipping the spear under my arm and grasping the reins with my free hand. Around me the column was getting underway, moving alongside the trees, skirting round the bodies of the condemned which lay face to the ground in the reddened snow, their limbs akimbo like broken dolls. A little further on, we joined an intersecting path and I set my horse trotting, hooves flew in the virgin snow, spears struck the branches and rained sprays of snow, needles, and pinecones on us, I laughed and my men laughed with me, filled with joy by this impromptu evening race through the woods. Further on opened up vast snowy fields, striped with the brown of tilled earth, we crossed them without slowing down, the snow was no longer falling, the sky was veering grey and growing darker, little by little the clouds unraveled, spilling over the tranquility of the countryside the white light of the full moon. Finally night settled in and I slowed the horses down to a walk. We moved through fields to the jangling of harnesses and spurs, the snorts of the horses, the muted sound of dozens of hooves in the snow, wrapped in the rich smells of frozen earth, leather, gun oil, horse sweat, and manure. The moon now illuminated everything, we could clearly make out the white and undulating expanses interspersed with little woods, slightly darker masses scattered here and there under the bluish vault of the nighttime sky. In the distance lights were shining, and without a word I headed the column toward them. Little by little, the forms of a great building took shape in front of us, nestled in trees and surrounded by outbuildings, an isolated manor like so many still left in these lands. A dog, alerted by our approach, began barking, followed by another, more lights came on and we heard brief shouts and the sound of doors. With a gesture of my spear, I sent two groups of men to flank the house as I continued to advance at a walk, followed by the bulk of the troop. Having reached the large gate of the enclosure, built of strong metal-trimmed wood, I knocked on it with my spear and cried: "Open up!" The dogs were barking louder, no one answered. "Open up! Open up or I'll burn everything down!" Finally a voice made itself heard: "Who goes there?"—"Open up, in the name of God," I growled, "if you care for your life." Finally the hinges grated and the heavy doors swung open. An older man appeared, holding up a lantern: "Who are you? What do you want?" Without taking the trouble to answer I sent my spear into his throat; his voice strangled in the blood, the lantern fell into the snow where it continued to shine, he remained suspended for an instant on the spear, until I twisted the shaft a little to free it. The corpse slipped onto the snow in turn and I shook the spear to clean it off; then I planted it in the ground and dismounted, tying my horse's tether to it. I didn't have to say anything, my men knew their work, I calmly lit another cigar and drew on it as they rushed toward the house, on foot or still on horseback. Gunshots rang out, one of them rolled onto the ground and stretched out full-length, the others knelt in the snow and opened fire, aiming for the windows, which burst one after the other in showers of glass. It was quickly over. A dozen soldiers rushed like mad dogs through the battered-in front door, some more gunshots rang out from inside, the sounds of doors flying into pieces, hoarse cries, the panicked screams of women. Leaving my horse there, I pulled my pistol out of its holster and went in, stepping over the body of a half-clothed young man whose blood was soaking the entry hall rug. Women in nightdresses were running down the halls, pursued by laughing soldiers; in the living room, in the midst of overturned furniture and corpses sprawled like puppets, an old man was sitting in his armchair, his eyes wide open, his lower lip trembling. All of a sudden, all the electric lights went out, the fuses must have blown, but the lighted candles and lanterns were enough to illuminate the scene. A sharp smell of cordite and blood filled my nose and I sniffed it with delight. In the outbuildings, a soldier was raping a fat maid on a table, under the laughing eyes of his comrades, another, calmly seated on a chair, was cutting slices of bread and cheese; two men overturned a sideboard filled with dishes, which collapsed in an immense racket of broken porcelain. A few gunshots still sounded in the back of the house; in the rear courtyard, behind the outbuildings, three soldiers, swearing, were struggling to bleed a pig, which squealed and fought with all its strength under the knife; near them, two ill-shaven peasants were being hoisted onto a cart, their hands tied behind their backs, to be hanged from a large oak tree; further on a barn was blazing, cheerfully. I went up to the second floor: the same joyful chaos reigned here, a sergeant, champagne flute in hand, was dancing alone in front of a large mirror hugging his own shoulders, a soldier was pissing into the drapes, a third was displaying hands covered in women's rings and bracelets. From a half-open door came piercing cries: two men, pants lowered, were screwing a naked boy bent forward on an iron bed, his head buried in the embroidered cushions. Further on, in the back of the hallway, there was a closed door. I tried the handle, the door was locked, I knocked, no reply, I knocked again with my fist and shouted "Open up!", still nothing. So I stepped back and kicked in the lock. The door flew open; standing in front of the bed was a woman wearing a pearl-grey house dress, thin and light, her Venetian blond hair done up in an artfully disheveled bun lit now by the wan light of the moon falling through the windowpanes. When she saw me she cried out and brought her hand to her mouth. "You!" she moaned. "You? But you are mad! You are mad!" I looked at her, puzzled by these words: "We don't know each other," I said curtly, stepping forward and giving her a slap that sent her spinning onto the green and gold expanse of the embroidered bedspread. She curled up and began sobbing, scratching her beautiful contorted face with her nails. I pushed the door, took off my coat and then my belt which I placed on a chair, and approached the bed, undoing my jacket. The young woman tried to hit me with her heel, I caught her ankle, laughing, and twisted it, forcing her onto her belly. I caressed her buttocks under the silky material of the dress, a knit jersey without the slightest seam and lined in a fine pale pink silk, she yelled with all her strength, her face buried in the long green grass embroidered in the cloth, I struck her in the back with my fist and her shouts instantly stopped, and then I pushed the dress up to her hips and curtly lowered her panties, revealing a white, round ass. She was moaning now, "No, no, I beg you," I hit her again to shut her up, undid my fly, hauled myself onto the bed and, spreading her buttocks, entered her with a fierce thrust of my hips. She cried out shrilly one last time, then fell silent. I buried my hands, still gloved in white, in her disheveled bun and leaned with all my weight on her head, breathing in the fragrance of heather, moss, and almond that emanated from her hair. But she was dry and I didn't find the sensation very pleasant, I withdrew, spit several times on her anus, nestled in the midst of tufts of blond hairs, rubbed saliva on my glans and pushed in there, slowly this time, she still didn't emit a sound, sprawled in her grey dress on the verdant bedspread, her face hidden by her loose hair. I turned to the side: next to the half-open door stood a tall upright mirror, I could see my ass there, white in the moonlight, moving in and out between her long white thighs, pinned beneath my own. I slowed down, feasting on the spectacle, the woman, under my body, breathed with a whistling sound but kept silent, I hit her again, without really knowing why, then again, at each blow she choked but restrained herself from crying out, and this silence enraged me, I began strangling her, both my gloved hands squeezing on her neck, I felt her thighs go taut and struggle beneath me, her ass contracted and I came abruptly, emptying myself into her in long spurts before letting her go and rolling onto my back, spread full-length on the embroidered grass, my eyes closed. Next to me I could hear the woman hiccup, cough, swallow air convulsively. I opened my eyes and sat up, looking at my crotch, there were traces of shit on my member, I drew a section of the bedspread toward me to wipe myself off, then buttoned up again. The woman was still lying on her belly, her buttocks exposed, she was sobbing quietly now, biting the cloth of the bedspread to stifle the sound. I gave her a little slap on the behind and she immediately fell silent: "You can go now," I said to her. Her head turned away, she painfully straightened up onto her knees, pulling on the cloth of her dress to cover her behind; she stood up, stumbled, leaned on the edge of the bed, then bent over to pull her panties up under her dress. I could only see her profile. She was biting her lower lip and the moonlight played with the stray hairs on her neck. Then she looked at me, her wild eyes empty of all comprehension. I made a little sign to her with my finger and she staggered toward the door. I leaned toward the chair, took my pistol out of its holster, cocked it, and aimed at her neck. The shot sent her flying against the door, she collapsed on the rug in a grey, twisted mass, leaving long red trails on the polished wood. I put the weapon down next to me and fell onto my back, absent-mindedly stroking the thick embroidery of the bedspread with my gloved fingers.

When I woke up the sky was just beginning to grow pale. A few muffled noises could still be heard, glass being broken, a melancholy song. I straightened up and tried to light a bedside lamp, but the electricity still wasn't working. In front of the door, the dark mass of the woman's body looked like a pile of dirty laundry, thrown there to be carried away by the maids. I got up, lit a few candles, and began searching through the furniture, pocketing the jewelry and currency I found. In the drawer of the night table I found several pieces of photographs. These cut fragments represented a little blond boy; and even more than the arms of a man that showed now and then, it was the expression of the child, now concentrated, now frightened, now bursting with joy, that reflected the presence of the other person eliminated by the scissors, a presence that meant everything to him. I threw them on the floor, finished my search, and, pushing the corpse away with my boot, went out to join my men. Most of them, drunk, were sleeping in armchairs, on rugs or on tables, others were humming as they emptied the last bottles; in front of the main steps, more sober soldiers were already preparing for departure, tying bags of spoils or provisions to their saddles. I ordered four of them to go wake up and collect their comrades; then I had my horse brought out and gave the order for departure to those who were ready. Spears in hand or on our shoulders, we went through the gate, skirting round the corpse of the old man with the lantern, stiff in the snow. Day was dawning, the sky was grey, in front of us stretched out the muted white of snowy fields, scattered with the darker patches of copses. I urged my horse to a trot with my heel, the men followed, cheerful and laughing. In the distance, isolated on the white expanse, I could make out a little black point, and I directed my horse toward it. As I grew closer I could see it was a figure, the figure of a naked, blond little boy staggering in the snow. We quickly caught up with him and he faced us as we surrounded him, pale, shaking with cold, his legs stained with shit he had let flow without realizing it during his flight, and his features deformed by tears, cold and terror. All around him, my cavalrymen formed a wall of spears and closed faces. My horse stepped forward, the kid fell on his ass, moved back, staggered up, floundering in the snow mixed with shit, he was soiling himself again, his face twisted by sobs, I killed him with a swift stab of my spear to his chest, lifted him up a little, then threw him down like a marionette in the snow, to the coarse laughter of my men. Then I set my horse to a gallop through the plain, lifted by an exalted feeling of sovereign freedom, the cold air bit into my cheeks and lungs and I fed on it, I felt myself growing in my saddle until I became equal with the vast plain, the snow, and the sky above me. In the late afternoon we reached a railway station occupied by enemy forces. Most of my troops had joined us and we assaulted it on all sides, in a deluge of gunfire and incoherent shouts; the enemy had positioned a machine gun at the main angle of attack and it held us at bay for a long time, until one of my soldiers, crawling to the foot of the wall, managed to silence it with a grenade. Then there was a mad scramble. The survivors poured out through the doors, hands over their heads, my men pressed them against the station wall and shot them without a pause, I was one of the first to enter the building itself, pistol in hand, an enemy soldier was aiming his rifle at me and I killed him with a single shot, further on a wounded man was crawling and I finished him off as well, all around us resounded gunfire and the screams of the dying. At the end of the main room there was a door, I kicked it in, it opened onto an empty gallery that I crossed while undoing my coat and belt, at the end of the gallery there was another door, I let my pistol fall and took off my jacket, also throwing away my two white gloves, quickly I undid the rest of my clothes, keeping only my tracksuit and pulling on my sneakers, which I had kept in a pocket, already the door was open and as soon as I had crossed the threshold I began to run. It was dark here, I was disoriented and I slammed against the walls several times, finally I found a semblance of balance and was able to move forward regularly, breathing with ease, to the rhythm of my strides. But the hallway was curved, I couldn't manage to stay in the center and again my shoulder hit a wall, I thought I could make out darker spots, intersections perhaps or just cubbyholes, I avoided them as well as I could until a stronger impact than the others made me stumble, I slowed down but didn't stop running, finally I ended up in the locker room and quickly changed, adjusting my swim cap and passing through the swinging doors, they opened onto a large space full of the echoes of shouts and sounds of water, all blue and luminous and made even bigger by long mirrors framing it, mirrors in which I could glimpse only fragments of my body, fleeting and with no connection between them, I swayed, almost fell, then I pulled myself together and straightened up, my balance suddenly returned, my body found its center of gravity and, muscles tense, buttocks tight, I dove in straight as a spear, slicing with all my weight through the clear, cool water of the pool.